"My Sunday school teacher said that if you give your troubles to God, He will help you through them."

Lily smiled at the young boy. "She's absolutely right, Nate."

"I've been asking God for a mom *forever*. And when you found that dog? I talked to Him about that, too. No mom, no dog. 'Nuff said."

"God doesn't always answer with a 'yes,' Nate, but He always answers," she explained. "Maybe he's saying 'Wait.' When the time's right, if it's His will…"

"His will? What's that?"

"Well, will is…it's like a plan. Long before you were born, God knew you, knew what was best for you, too. And for as long as you live, He'll do everything in His power to see that you have what you need."

"What I need is a mom." And under his breath, "Dog would be nice, too."

Oh, if only *she* could fill that role! He was adorable, big-hearted, smarter than any four-year-old she'd ever met. And he was part of his father. No ~~wonder she~~ ~~~~ ~~~~ y about him!

Books by Loree Lough

Steeple Hill Love Inspired

*Suddenly Daddy #28
*Suddenly Mommy #34
*Suddenly Married #52
*Suddenly Reunited #107
*Suddenly Home #130
His Healing Touch #163
Out of the Shadows #179
†An Accidental Hero #214
†An Accidental Mom #225

*Suddenly!
†Accidental Blessings

LOREE LOUGH

A full-time writer for many years, Loree Lough has produced more than two thousand articles, dozens of short stories and novels for the young (and young at heart), and all have been published here and abroad. The award-winning author of more than thirty-five romances, Loree also writes as Cara McCormack and Aleesha Carter.

A comedic teacher and conference speaker, Loree loves sharing in classrooms what she's learned the hard way. The mother of two grown daughters, she lives in Maryland with her husband and an old-as-dirt cat named Mouser (who, until she caught and killed her first mouse, had no idea what a rodent was).

AN ACCIDENTAL MOM

LOREE LOUGH

Love Inspired.

Published by Steeple Hill Books

STEEPLE HILL BOOKS

Steeple
Hill®

ISBN 0-373-87232-1

AN ACCIDENTAL MOM

Printed in U.S.A.

I will sing the mercies of the Lord forever;
with my mouth I will make known thy faithfulness
to all generations.

—*Psalms* 89:1

To Larry, without whose patience and
understanding my writing wouldn't be possible;
to Elice and Valerie, my daughters and best friends.

Chapter One

The four-year-old wrapped an arm around his father's leg. "Daddy," he said, tugging at the pocket of his father's sports coat, "why do people come to the simmy-terry?"

The day was as gray as Max Sheridan's mood, and Nate's questions did nothing to improve it. He looked into the innocent, brown eyes and smiled despite himself. Oh, but he loved this kid! "To visit loved ones, Nate. To pay our respects to people who have died."

Nate knelt in the damp grass. One by one, he placed the white roses he'd chosen at the flower mart at the feet of the marble angel guarding his mother's grave. "Mommy isn't in there." He spoke with conviction. "Only her bones. Her soul is in heaven with God."

He stood and pressed close to his father. "Right, Dad?"

Max inhaled deeply. "Yes, Nate." He'd told bedtime stories to soothe the boy to sleep; how different was *this* white lie? He'd tried believing in God, in miracles. Well, if God truly existed and He could perform miracles, he and Nate wouldn't be here at Melissa's grave, now would they?

For a long time, Nate merely stared at the tombstone. "She isn't cold, you know...."

Nate had been too young when Melissa died to have any real memory of her. He seemed to have no recollection of those bleak days in the funeral parlor, when friends and relatives speculated about why a beautiful woman with so much to live for would take her own life. If there had been a God to thank for that, Max would have prayed himself hoarse. Max had only brought Nate to Peaceful Gardens twice, and each visit inspired new curiosities—and childlike observations about death, dying and the afterlife—in his son.

"...because the tempa-chure in heaven is always a pleasant seventy-five degrees." Nate's beaming face told Max how proud he was to have remembered that tidbit of information.

Max chuckled. He was something else, this kid of his. "Where'd you hear that?"

"Gramma Georgia tol' me so, on the phone yesterday when I tol' her we were coming here to say goodbye to Mommy. She said Mommy will always be warm and happy, 'cause everything is *perfect* up in heaven."

If God didn't exist, then neither did heaven. But Max smiled. He saw no point in tarnishing the boy's image of...things.

Even Max didn't understand why, when in all other

areas he'd been a no-nonsense, tell-it-like-it-is parent. Fairy tales were stories, nothing more. Santa and the Easter Bunny were invented to put money into the pockets of the greeting card manufacturers. The tooth fairy? The lazy parents' way of coaxing their kids to brush and floss. Far better to extinguish his son's belief in fantasies like that than to let him grow up and find out how painful and unrelenting the real world could be.

Strangely, though, he was less rigid when it came to matters of religion, spirituality and faith. If Nate wanted to attend Sunday school with his school chums, fine. If he wanted to tag along when the neighbors attended services, so be it. Nate got so much out of the whole "church thing" that Max couldn't bring himself to put an end to it. Something, though, told him that the longer he waited to teach the boy the truth as he saw it, the more difficult it would be.

"Is Gramma full of beans?"

Laughing, Max took Nate's hand. Where did the kid come up with this stuff? "'Course not, son."

Nate's face crinkled with confusion. "But, Dad, you said so yourself, just last night, 'member?"

Yes, he remembered, only too well. He'd been on the phone with his mother, discussing the trip to Amarillo, when she started with her usual "bless this" and "pray for that" nonsense. Max's day had been bad enough to that point; being forced to listen to her spiritual malarkey was the proverbial straw on the camel's already overloaded back. "If your precious Lord is so merciful," he'd demanded, "why'd He allow Melissa to take her own life? Why'd He let you—a woman who devoted her whole life to Him—break your leg?''

''I didn't raise you to talk like that!'' Georgia had scolded. And when she started praying for his salvation, he'd put a hand over the phone and closed his eyes. ''Mom,'' he'd muttered, ''you're full of beans.''

And that's when he'd noticed Nate, standing in the doorway.

''I was only teasing,'' Max had whispered past the phone's mouthpiece. ''Besides, Gramma didn't hear me.''

But Nate's doubting expression said he believed otherwise.

Now, Nate stood and brushed freshly mowed grass clippings from the knees of his jeans. ''You gonna say goodbye to Mommy, Dad?''

Closing his eyes, Max held his breath and summoned the strength to go through the motions…for Nate. He'd tried to say goodbye to Melissa, for even as the EMTs struggled to save her, they'd known she was dying. Instead, he'd struggled to keep a lid on his temper. Max couldn't remember being more angry with her. He hadn't understood why she left Nate then, and he didn't understand it now…nearly three years later.

The very people who, when he was a boy, taught him that suicide was one of the most grievous sins a human could commit, also believed that God in His heaven had total control over things on earth, that He loved every last person. If that was true, why did some of His ''children'' die of starvation, while others became victims of genocide and war? Why did good people get cancer, while bad people robbed and raped and pillaged?

Despite all that, their simple faith seemed to bring them such joy, such solace. Nate—more than any of them, Max believed—deserved to grow up feeling that way. At least until life stepped in and taught him otherwise in its usual fist-to-jaw way.

"You gonna say a prayer for Mommy?"

Prayer. Of all the— Groaning inwardly, Max shaded his eyes. "Tell you what," he said from behind his hand, "why don't *you* say the prayer this time."

"Me?" Nate's brown eyes widened. "Thanks, Dad! I'll do a good job. I promise." He got down on his knees and bowed his head, then he closed his eyes and pressed both palms together, fingers pointing skyward. "God? It's me, Nathan Maxwell Sheridan. Um, me an' my dad won't be comin' to visit my mom here at the simmy-terry for a while, on accounta my gramma busted her leg an'—"

"Broke her leg," Max corrected gently. He didn't see much sense in correcting the "for a while" part.

"...on accounta Gramma broke her leg, an' we're going to Texas to take care of her 'til she can walk again. So, God? Could You do me a favor? I know my mom's soul is up there in heaven with You, so maybe You could tell her not to worry 'bout her bones an' her wedding ring an' stuff while we're gone, 'cause the men who work here take real good care of the place. Thanks." Nate started to get up, then changed his mind. Eyes squinted tight-shut again, he added, "And, God? Please send another wife for my dad…and a mom for me. We really, *really* need one. Amen."

On his feet again, Nate put his hand into Max's. "How was that, Dad? Did I do good?"

Max swallowed the hard lump that always formed in his throat when Nate prayed for a new mom. It was only natural, he supposed, that even though Nate didn't remember Melissa, he'd yearn for a mother's love. But he was doing okay by the boy, wasn't he? Hadn't he learned to cook—a little? Hadn't he taught himself to do laundry—sort of? He'd figured out every gizmo on that fancy vacuum cleaner of Melissa's—hadn't he? And tough as it had been to go it alone, he hadn't missed a single Parents' Night at Nate's school. What did they need a woman for!

Max hoisted his son, held him close. "You did great with that prayer, kiddo, just great. Now whatsay you and I head over to the burger joint. We have enough time for chicken fingers and curly fries before we head out."

Nate kissed Max's cheek. "You're the best, Dad. Almost as good as havin' a mom *and* a dad!"

Almost as good, Max thought, *but not quite.* Sad fact was, Nate would never have it "as good"—at least, not in the mom department, because Max had made a promise to himself when Melissa died.

And he aimed to keep it.

"Well, as I live and breathe," Georgia said, slapping the arm of her wheelchair. "If it isn't Lily London!"

"Oh, my!" Lily said, pointing at the woman's cast. "What have you done to yourself?"

The redhead smiled. "One leg too few in a three-legged race?"

"Don't let her pull *your* leg, Lily," the fry cook called over the counter. "Genius Georgia was changing lightbulbs...on a stool with wheels." He raised floured hands and shook his head. "Again!"

Georgia waved his comment away. "Oh, put a lid on it, Andy." As an aside to Lily, she added in a loud whisper, "That man doesn't know what he's talkin' about."

"I know what I saw," Andy argued.

Lily scooted a chrome and vinyl-padded chair nearer to Georgia's wheelchair. "Is that cast as uncomfortable as it looks?"

"Nah. Hardest part about wearin' this thing," she said, knocking on the toes-to-thigh plaster, "is not being able to get around like I'd like to."

"How long 'til you're back on your feet?"

"Ten weeks. Eight, if I'm very, very good." Georgia tucked a red curl behind her ear. "One good thing came of it, though."

"In other words," Andy tossed in, "ten weeks. Probably more!"

Georgia feigned a frown. "Funny man. Maybe we oughta get you a gig at the local comedy club."

Lily helped herself to a cup of coffee. "Can I get you some?"

"Had my quota for the day, thanks."

"So, what's the 'good thing' to come of your broken leg?"

"Max is coming home," Georgia said, beaming. "And he's bringing little Nate with him!"

Lily felt as though her heart had plummeted into her stomach. Max? Coming back to Amarillo? She put her coffee on the counter, afraid her trembling might cause her to spill it. "When…um…when will Max be here?"

Georgia glanced at her wristwatch. "They called from the road not half an hour ago, so they should roll in here any—"

The door burst open and a small boy with curly brown hair exploded into Georgia's diner. He was the spitting image of Max, right down to the adorable dimples bracketing his wide grin.

"Gramma!" he squealed, arms outstretched as he ran toward Georgia. "Gramma, we're finally here!"

Georgia hugged him tight, then held his rosy-cheeked face in her hands. "Lemme have a look at my favorite grandson," she said, pressing a noisy kiss to his chin.

Giggling, Nate said, "How can I be your favorite grandson when I'm your *only* grandson?" He swiped at the spot his grandmother had kissed. "And second, how can you have a look at me while you're *kissin'* me!"

His grandmother hugged him again. "Four-year-old genius," she told Lily, "just like his daddy. Yes'm. That's my boy!"

She glanced toward the door. "Speaking of which, where *is* your daddy?"

"Parking the car." Nate's eyes widened. "You

should see all the squished bugs on the front bumper. Must be a million of 'em!''

As Georgia laughed, Lily smiled self-consciously. She had to get out of here, fast, because it would be only a matter of seconds before the genius's father followed him into the diner. And she had no desire to see Max Sheridan again, not after—

"Actually," Nate added, "it isn't 'zactly a car. It's an Ess Yoo Vee. It's big and red, like a fire truck. He bought it right before you busted your leg."

"*Broke* my leg," Georgia corrected. "I still think you and your dad should have flown into town, saved all those hours on the road. Especially considering there's a perfectly good car in the garage that he could've—"

"I'm a pencil pusher, not Mr. America," interrupted a teasing baritone. "What makes you think I could steer that boat of yours?"

It was Max, looking more gorgeous than Lily remembered. Tall and broad-shouldered, he seemed more at ease with himself than when she'd last seen him, more manly and mature. Marriage had done that to him, she supposed. Marriage and fatherhood.

Lily swallowed the lump of jealousy that formed in her throat and asked God to forgive her pettiness, because much as she'd wanted to be the one at his side when those things happened, he'd chosen someone else.

"Max!" Georgia waved him over. "C'mere and give your old fat mama a great big hug!"

He crossed the room in three long strides and bent

to wrap his mother in a warm embrace. "First...
you're not fat."

"I hope you're gonna say 'Second...you're not
old.'" She gave him a playful poke in the ribs.

"Do you see 'Fool' tattooed to my forehead?" He
assumed a serious stance and a pious expression.

They enjoyed a laugh, then Georgia said, "You
know my motto."

"'God and Nature have decreed that I will age,'"
Max quoted, "'...but I refuse to get *old!*'"

He crouched beside the footrest of her chair. "So,
let's have a look at this leg of yours."

While Max inspected his mother's cast, Lily did
her best to sneak out of the diner unnoticed.

"Stop right there!" Georgia hollered.

Lily froze in her tracks, only too aware that all eyes
were now on her. Caught in the act!

"Where d'you think you're going, young lady?
You can't leave 'til you put your John Hancock on
my leg!"

Feeling the heat of a blush creep into her cheeks,
Lily moved woodenly toward the wheelchair.
"Sorry," she said, accepting Georgia's felt-tipped
pen. "Where would you like me to—"

"Daddy," interrupted Nate's hoarse whisper. He
tugged at his father's hand. "She's *bee-yoo-tee-ful!*"

Lily chanced a quick glance in Max's direction.
Now he was blushing. Her heartbeat doubled when
he met her eyes and smiled that oh-so-tantalizing half
grin that had captivated her years ago. She'd changed
a lot since he left for Chicago; she hoped he wouldn't
recognize her.

He got to his feet. "Lily? Lily London?"

Yeah, she thought bitterly, *it's me. The silly little twit who used to tag along behind you like a well-trained puppy, hoping for a pat on the head.* She plastered what she hoped was a sophisticated smile on her face and tried to sound composed.

"How are you, Max?"

How long had it been since she last saw him? Five years? No, six…if she didn't count the tens of thousands of times she'd pictured him in her dreams. Six long years since he'd left Amarillo—with his blushing bride on his arm.

"Wow. Look at you! I hardly recognized you. It's great to see you."

If he'd given her a thought at all in all these years—which was doubtful—he'd probably pictured her in braces and a ponytail, and carrying an armload of books. Surely the change hadn't been *that* drastic, so why was he staring at her as if she had a third eye in the middle of her forehead?

Lily broke the intense eye contact by pretending to recap the pen, but ended up stabbing her palm with the point, instead.

She stifled an *ouch,* as Georgia said, "Who'da thunk that skinny freckle-faced li'l gal would grow up to be such a knockout!"

Nate took a step closer and smiled up at her. She'd heard through the grapevine that Max and Melissa had had a son. Mostly, she'd tried not to think about the fact that Max had started a life with someone other than her, because she'd loved him almost from the first moment they'd met—when she was a knobby-kneed seventh grader and he'd been Centennial High School's star quarterback.

"Hi," the boy said. "My name is Nathan Maxwell Sheridan. Max, here, is my dad. I'm very pleased to make your awk-a-ah…"

"Acquaintance," his father helped.

"That's it," Nate said, nodding, "'acquaintance.'" He looked up into Lily's face. "What's your name?"

"Her name is Lily," Georgia said. "Lily London."

"Sounds like a movie star's name." He furrowed his brow. "But I thought a lily was a flower."

"It is," Lily said, shrugging. "My mother's name was Rose, see, so I guess she thought it would be neat to name my sisters and me after flowers."

Nate giggled. "That's pretty funny." He giggled again. "What're your sisters' names?"

"The twins are Ivy and Violet, and there's Cammi…which is short for Camellia."

He narrowed his big, black-lashed eyes. "They're nice names, but I like Lily best."

A person would have to be made of stone not to warm to this child, she admitted, mirroring his friendly grin. "Well, thanks, Nate," she said, shaking his extended hand. "And I'm pleased to make your acquaintance, too."

He jerked a thumb over his shoulder. "My dad here could sure use a wife. See, my mom died when I was a baby. He does pretty good, considering he's not a lady, but he sure could use some help. So…are you married?"

Georgia chuckled under her breath as Max slapped a hand over his eyes and gave a loud sigh.

Lily found herself enjoying his discomfort, perhaps a little too much. "I'm afraid I'm a little too busy to…help your dad out. I have a job. Two, in fact."

His brows nearly met in the center of his forehead. "Wow. *Two* jobs?" he said, stuffing both hands into his pants pockets.

As if on cue, Max did the same thing, Lily noticed. It was obvious the two spent a lot of time together, because Nate had also picked up Max's tendency to say "first" this and "second" that. Maybe Nate hadn't been too far from the mark when he'd said Max was an okay parent.

"I'm an animal rehabilitator," she told the boy. "And I manage my father's ranch."

Nate's brow furrowed. "What's that?"

"She nurses sick and injured animals back to health," Max explained, "then takes them back where they came from." To Lily, he added, "Sorry. He's a great kid, but sometimes he talks too much."

She was about to agree that Nate was a great kid and add that Max had nothing to apologize for, when Nate said, "Your dad has a ranch? With horses and cows and stuff?"

Lily smiled again. "He sure does."

"Man, I've never been on a real-live ranch before. They don't have 'em in Chicago, y'know."

She glanced at Max. He'd grown up in cattle country; why hadn't he taken the boy to see his buddies' homes during visits to his mother?

"Are you a vettin-air-yun?"

"No, Nate, but I do work very closely with one."

He crossed both arms over his chest. "I'm gonna

be a vettin-air-yun when I grow up, 'cause I like animals.''

"Do you, now? Do you have a cat or a dog?"

Nate shot his father a less-than-friendly look. "Dad says I'm not old enough to be 'sponsible for a pet."

"Well, maybe you'd like to come out to our ranch sometime, see my animals."

Nate gasped. "Really? I could do that? Cool! What kind of animals!"

"Oh, a raccoon and a wolf cub, an eagle, some hawks, three monkeys and—"

"Monkeys! *Way* cool! Dad, I wanna—"

One look into his father's stern face was enough to silence the boy. Lily couldn't help but wonder why Max would have a problem with Nate visiting River Valley. It was the most natural thing in the world for a city boy to get enthused about the prospect of seeing animals up close, especially if his only prior contact had been at Chicago's Brookfield Zoo!

Lily knew that if she didn't get out of there fast, she'd likely say something she'd regret. "Where should I sign?" she asked Georgia, pen poised above the cast.

Georgia pointed, and Lily scribbled *Get Well Quick!* above her signature. "I'd love to stay and chat," she fibbed, handing Georgia her pen, "but I have a million things to do."

"You got any kids?" Nate asked.

"No," Lily told him. "But with two jobs, I don't have time to properly take care of children." She didn't tell him that not being able to make her "wife and mommy" dream come true was one of the most disappointing and heartbreaking facts of her life. The lump that formed in her throat surprised her.

And before any of them could say another word, she headed for the door. "Bye," she called over her shoulder. "See you all later."

Not! she tacked on as the door hissed shut behind her. At least, not if she had anything to say about it!

During the drive back to the ranch, Lily's cell phone rang. "There's a dog doing its best to keep from drowning in Lake Meredith," her sister said. "I heard two small-craft pilots talking about it, listening to my CB radio. They've been hovering overhead for a couple minutes. Don't know how long the poor thing has been down there. If someone doesn't do something for it soon, one of 'em is gonna put it out of its misery—with a rifle!"

The mental picture of a dog paddling like mad to stay afloat, while sharpshooters zeroed in on it, made Lily's heart flinch. Ordinarily, she didn't specialize in household pets but this was hardly an ordinary circumstance. "Okay, all right, calm down before you fall down," Lily said, making a quick U-turn on Route 40. "I'm on my way. Meanwhile, get back on that CB of yours and see if you can reach those guys. Tell the trigger-happy one to keep the safety on his weapon. I'll be there in less than an hour."

She'd witnessed situations like this before, and knew that unless the dog had been injured, it could stay afloat for an amazingly long time. Over the years, people had taken to calling her Snow White because of her talent for communicating with animals. She hoped the gift would help her coax this poor pup to the shore before...

Taking the exit onto Route 136 and heading north to the small town of Fritch, Lily forced the horrifying image from her mind. *Lord, get me there fast,* she prayed. "Say, Vi..."

"Hmm?"

"I've always wondered...why do you have a CB radio in your shop?"

Violet laughed. "Well, originally I got it to keep track of deliveries. If a deliveryman called to say he was stuck in traffic, I'd know within minutes if he was telling the truth or feeding me a line of baloney. Didn't take long to weed the dishonest ones from those I could trust."

Grinning, Lily waited for the "other" reasons.

"I realized pretty quick it's also a great place to catch up on local gossip. *And* I find out when a busload of tourists is rolling in at Georgia's. One quick trip to the diner, one quiet mention of all the good deals across the street at my boutique, and I have all the business I can handle 'til the bus rolls out again."

Lily couldn't help but smile. "So much for the 'dumb blonde' adage. You're one of the savviest businesswomen I've ever known."

She listened to the heavy silence for a few seconds before saying, "Vi? You there?"

"Yeah. I was just thinking about that poor dog."

Nodding, Lily said, "Me, too. But don't worry. I'll do everything I can to save it."

"'Course you will. Why do you think I called you as soon as I heard about it!"

"I only hope the mutt is wearing tags, so I can reunite him with his owner fast as I can. This whole ordeal will be traumatic enough without being separated from loved ones."

"Well, a customer just walked in. Call mé later, let me know how things turned out."

Lily hung up, hoping that when "later" came, she wouldn't have to tell her sister she'd been forced to take the dog home. It wouldn't be the first time she'd taken in a lost dog or cat, and experience had taught her it wouldn't be the last. Whether bringing the animal back to its former healthy state took months or days, every situation lasted only long enough to roust out a good family to adopt the pet. But regardless of how much or how little time and energy she invested in the creatures, Lily always experienced a period of mourning while she adjusted to life without the furry critter.

Nate Sheridan came to mind, with his big brown eyes and mop of dark curls. If she managed to save the dog and couldn't find its owner, maybe...

Of course, that would require direct contact with Max. Lily's heart beat double time at the mere thought. Clucking her tongue, she whispered through clenched teeth, "Get a grip, girl." Because, really, what could happen between them in the few minutes it would take to get his permission to introduce Nate to the rescued dog?

"You're getting way ahead of yourself, Lily." She had no idea what kind of dog was splashing around for its life, no clue what condition it might be in by the time she reached it. A glance at her dashboard clock told her she'd been on the road less than fifteen minutes; it was nearly an hour's drive to the entrance gate at Lake Meredith.

It dawned on her suddenly that she hadn't asked Violet *where* the pilots had seen the dog. Acres of water made up this stretch of the park.

She reached for her cell phone, punched in her sister's code. "Hey, kiddo…it's me," she said when her sister answered. "I didn't think to ask earlier, but did those pilots mention where they spotted the dog?"

"I remember something about the boat dock. They thought maybe the dog had fallen off a sailboat or something."

"But who'd go boating at this time of year?"

"I know I wouldn't want to waste a nice day like this if I'd sunk a hundred grand into a sailboat."

Violet made a good point, Lily admitted. The weather had been remarkably balmy for October, these past few weeks. "Did you manage to raise either of them on your CB?"

"No. We must be on a weird frequency. I'm hearing them fine, but they didn't respond to me at all."

Just great! Lily thought. Chances were pretty good that the sharpshooter who'd talked himself into believing he'd be doing a good deed by "putting the dog out of its misery" might actually take aim…and pull the trigger!

"Thanks, Vi. I'd better step on it. I'm still forty-five minutes away. I'll call soon as I know something," she said, and hung up.

"Please, God," she said aloud, "watch over that

pup. Give him the strength he needs to hang on 'til I get there.''

Maybe she should phone Georgia, so she and Nate could join in her prayer. No, the kid would get his hopes up. And knowing how much danger the dog was in would only worry him. Besides, if she didn't reach the lake in time, his little heart would break, and for what? Lily knew only too well how much it hurt to lose an animal, any animal.

''Help me, Lord....''

What if she phoned ahead, told the rangers at the gate who she was! If she described her car and explained the urgency of her mission, they'd let her through without stopping.

Lily said a quick thank you to the Almighty for the idea and grabbed the phone again, dialed the number she'd memorized ages ago—and stomped on the gas.

Chapter Two

"Here's our very own TV star!" Georgia said when Lily walked into the diner. "Does your dad know what got you on the evening news *this* time?"

"No, thankfully." Lily plopped onto a stool at the counter and sighed. "But I'll have to keep him away from television, at least 'til this whole 'daring rescue' nonsense is old news."

Georgia clucked her tongue. "In all fairness to the reporters, from what I saw, you *did* risk your life to save that mutt."

Shrugging, Lily rolled her eyes. "I borrowed a rowboat and paddled to the middle of Lake Meredith. Hardly what I'd call life-threatening."

"Yeah. Right. Without knowing if the dog was vicious, or diseased." She punctuated her opinion with a haughty *harrumph*. The redhead aimed a bony forefinger at Lily. "You can't fool an old fool, so quit tryin', girlie!"

Then Georgia's brow furrowed. "How'd the soggy

ol' fleabag get out in the middle of the lake in the first place?''

Grinning, Lily shrugged again. Leave it to Georgia to put a brand-new spin on things. ''Near as anyone can figure, she fell off a boat. When her leash got tangled in a buoy wire, she couldn't get loose.'' She frowned. ''Guess her collar fell off in the struggle. Weird thing is, none of the boaters on the lake claimed her.''

''Maybe she didn't fall. Maybe somebody tossed her overboard.''

Lily gasped. ''Why would anyone do such a horrible thing! Especially considering she's a beautiful, well-behaved, intelligent golden retriever.''

''Maybe she has the mange.''

''There isn't a single solitary thing wrong with her. She's positively perfect.''

Georgia leaned closer and whispered beside a cupped palm. ''Maybe she witnessed a murder and the killer had to get rid of her so she couldn't identify him.''

Lily laughed. ''That would be pretty spectacular, even for a dog as smart as Missy.''

''Oh, ho! Don't be so quick to judge. I read a novel where a dog could communicate by spelling stuff, using Scrabble tiles. Now *that* was one brilliant canine.'' She narrowed her eyes. ''Hey, wait just a minute. Did you call her 'Missy'?''

Lily nodded.

''I thought she didn't have a collar.''

Another shrug. ''She didn't. But, how she got into

the lake, who owns her, her medical history—it's all a mystery. So I called her Miss-Terry.''

"Miss-Terry, I get it," Georgia said. "Missy for short." Then she added, "Not the smartest move you've ever made."

Lily held up one hand. "I know, I know. If I do find her family, it'll be harder to give her up now, because I named her." But then, it always was hard to give up an animal once she'd rehabilitated it. Eagles and hawks, lizards and snakes, fawns…it didn't matter what species; Lily inevitably went through a period of mourning when her work with the animal was done.

She glanced at Georgia's cast. "What's this I hear about your leg not healing properly, about your needing surgery?"

"Where'd you hear that?"

"One of the park rangers is married to your doctor's receptionist. She called on his cell phone while we were debating how to save Missy. He mentioned my name, and she wanted to know if I was the girl who used to waitress at Georgia's Diner. I said no, that was my sister, Cammi. And she asked if he'd heard about your leg."

Georgia stared in silence for a moment. "Well, I guess it's true what they say."

"Bad news travels like wildfire?"

"'Zactly."

"So," Lily pressed, "what does the doctor hope to accomplish with an operation?"

It was Georgia's turn to shrug. "Oh, who knows? Robert probably wants to do it so he can pay off that fancy sports car of his." Chuckling, she added, "Either that, or he wasn't kidding when he said the bone isn't knitting like it's supposed to." She shook her head. "Says he'll have to put a pin or two in there, hold things in place."

Lily patted her hand. "I'll add you to my prayer list. That'll get the job done." She gave Georgia a look. "'Robert'?"

Georgia blushed but ignored the question. "So tell me, what brings you to town? It isn't like you to stay away from your menagerie so long."

"Well," Lily began, looking left and right, "I wanted to run an idea by you. If you agree, maybe I can solicit your help."

"Oooh," the woman said, rubbing both hands together. "Sounds like a conspiracy. Count me in!"

"Hear me out, first. You might decide it's the worst idea since Custer took his last stand."

"Then, time's a-wastin', girl. Spit it out!"

Lily told Georgia about her plan to unite the golden retriever with Nate. "Missy has such a sweet-natured temperament. If Max will allow it, she'd be great company for Nate."

Georgia pursed her lips, chin resting on a bent forefinger, considering the idea. "Y'know, I think you're right." She met Lily's eyes. "There's plenty of space in my apartment, even for a dog Missy's size. It's just the three of us, after all, rattling around in six big rooms." She nodded. "I think it's a terrific idea. That poor li'l guy hasn't had it easy, being alone with Max since his mama died."

The mere mention of Max's wife made Lily bristle,

waking feelings of jealousy. She felt petty and silly, too, because Max had never so much as given her the time of day. "If I'm not being too personal, how did his…" She struggled to get the word out. "How did his wife die?"

"Killed herself. Pills."

Georgia said it so matter-of-factly, Lily didn't know how to react. "Suicide? But, why?" With a man like Max for a husband, and a son as great as Nate, why would any woman in her right mind—

"She never was wrapped too tight," Georgia said as if she'd read Lily's mind. "A bubble off plumb, as my daddy used to say." She gave a dismissive wave of her hand. "I told Max she'd be trouble, but would he listen? Nooo. He had to be the big brave hero, try and rescue her."

"From what?"

"That's just it. The girl was born with a silver spoon in her mouth. Her mama took her to New York every summer, to outfit her for school. She'd do just about anything to be the center of attention. Guess when li'l Nate came along and stole her thunder, she just plain couldn't handle it." Crossing both arms over her chest, Georgia shook her head. "Spoiled brat, if you ask me."

"Did she…did she leave a note?"

"But, of *course*." Sarcasm rang loud in Georgia's voice. "How better to command center stage again, even if it had to be from the grave! She made good and sure Max would spend the rest of his life blaming himself for her death. And so far, she's succeeded."

"What do you mean, she succeeded?"

"First, he hasn't been out on a date since before he met her. And second, he won't go anywhere or do anything that might even *hint* at having fun. As if that's not bad enough, he's totally given up on God."

Well, that explained the ever-so-serious expression on his handsome face. Explained his stern attitude toward Nate, too. "Sad," Lily said. "He used to be so goofy, such fun, the life of every party."

"Which is *exactly* why I think you had a doggone good idea, if you'll pardon the pun."

Lily forced herself to grin. "You really think Max will go for it?"

"You 'n' me will see that he does!"

"Just so he doesn't see it as interfering…"

"How could he see you matching his son up with a great dog like Missy as interference?" Georgia laughed. "You add my leg to your prayer list, I'll add Max's answer to mine."

"Deal!" Lily said, shaking the woman's hand.

Neither of them noticed the three-foot tall shadow standing near the bottom of the stairs.…

Nate's dad had scolded him enough times for thundering down the steps. This time, he was determined to get to the first floor as quietly as possible. So he pretended to be an Indian brave, stalking a deer in the forest. "Heap big bunch of meat," he whispered, remembering the Daniel Boone movie he'd seen earlier. "Take home to squaw." He raised the plastic shovel-turned-tomahawk just as he reached the bottom step…just in time to hear Lily and his grandmother talking about getting a dog!

He snuck back up to the second floor and slipped into his room. *A dog!* he thought as his sneakered foot hit the top step. A dog named Missy. Nate didn't give a thought to the color of her fur, her age, the loudness of her bark. His only thought was a dog that he would soon have of his very own!

Flopping onto his back on the twin bed that was his here in Amarillo, he kicked both feet into the air and punched the mattress. "Yippee!" he whispered.

"Gramma, how old does a person have to be to use the telephone?"

"Old enough to talk, I guess," she said distractedly.

Nate watched as she filed her fingernails. "What if a person wants to talk to somebody, but he doesn't know their number?"

"He could look the number up in the phone book...."

Slapping a hand to his forehead, Nate did his best not to appear impatient. "But what if the person can't read?"

"Then, I guess he'd have to call Information."

"Information?"

His grandmother nodded. "He'd have to dial four-one-one and tell the nice lady what city and state the person he wants to call lives in."

"We're in Amarillo, Texas, right?"

"Right."

Now he watched as Georgia shook a tiny bottle of fingernail polish. "You gonna paint your nails, Gramma?"

"Mmm-hmm."

"Why? 'Cause that nice man is coming over again tonight?" Nate thought she looked right pretty, not at all like a grandmother, when she smiled like that.

He was about to tell her so, when she said, "He's going to load me into his car and take me out to eat. And then we're going to the movies."

"Cool. Whatcha gonna see?"

"Who knows? Something funny, I expect. Robert loves comedies."

Nate nodded, mirroring Georgia's frown as she concentrated on layering each fingernail with a coat of pearly white polish. "So Gramma…"

"Hmm?"

"After this person tells the nice lady what city and state, then what?"

"Then he tells her the name of the person who lives in that city and state, and she recites the phone number. Unless it's unlisted."

"'Recites'?"

"Tells," Georgia clarified. "She tells him the person's phone number."

Nate could read better than most four-year-olds, but not nearly well enough, he knew, to look someone up in the telephone directory. He could write his numbers, though, because his dad had started teaching him as soon as he could hold on to a colored marker.

He was thankful that his grandmother's focus was still on *her* hand. And his dad was down the street, buying washers to repair the leaking kitchen faucet. If God had been listening when he'd asked for assistance, Nate could make the call before either of them could say their favorite word: *Whippersnapper.*

"What's for supper, Gramma?" he asked, heading for the stairs.

"I think your dad said something about fixing chicken fingers for the two of you." Suddenly, she tucked her tongue between her top and bottom lip. "What do you expect," she muttered to herself, "when you've only used nail polish twice in your entire life!"

"I *love* chicken fingers. 'Specially with honey-and-mustard dippin' sauce."

"Mmm-hmm…"

"God?" Nate whispered as he climbed the stairs. "Help me remember everything Gramma just said, okay?"

Closing the apartment door quietly behind him, the boy sat on the end of the couch nearest the telephone. Holding the handset to his head, he pressed *four-one-one.*

"And, God?" he continued, waiting for the numbers to connect him to the nice lady. "Let Dad say yes about Missy the dog!"

Lily rather liked the way Missy followed her around. The dog sat quietly as Lily fed milk to a baby squirrel. And while she cleaned the eagle's cage, Missy lay quietly, head resting on her forepaws, cinnamon-brown eyes watching every move. It was as though the retriever understood that the barn was both shelter and hospital for birds with broken wings, for orphaned bunnies…for dogs who'd been separated from their families.

"You're a pretty cool mutt," she said, ruffling the golden fur. "Even Obnoxious thinks so!" Missy got along well with her dad's dog. Surprising in itself, because while Obnoxious had never been vicious, he'd never before befriended one of Lily's visiting canines.

Missy sat on her haunches and sent Lily a happy-doggy grin. She was about to admit that if Max said Nate couldn't have a dog, she'd keep Missy for herself—but the phone rang, forestalling her speech.

"Miss Lily?"

Nate? But why would he be phoning *her?* "Yes."

"It's me, Nathan Maxwell Sheridan. We met at my gramma's diner?"

Lily grinned. "Yes, I remember." How could she forget, when he'd plied her with compliments and practically asked her to be his mother! "How nice to hear from you, Nate."

"I just called to say thanks for saving that dog today. You're not just pretty, you're brave, too."

He was his father's son, all right, adept at flirting, even at the tender age of four. Max had made an art form of it in high school. Surely he'd only improved since—

Lily remembered what Georgia had said—that Max hadn't dated, had practically refused to do anything that involved a good time since his wife's death.

"I heard you, a little while ago, telling Gramma that you want me to have the dog. So I'm calling to make sure you know I'll take *very* good care of her.

I'll be nice to her and I'll keep her clean and I'll feed her on time every day and I'll take her for walks. I *promise*.''

If it was possible to hug a person through the phone, Lily would have hugged Nate, just for being his adorable, sincere self. ''I'm sure you'll be a wonderful master for Missy,'' Lily said. She was about to explain that the dog could only be his with his dad's approval, when Nate spoke.

''I'm very gentle, you know. I don't pull dogs' ears or tails, like some kids do. I don't tease them, either, because, well, teasing isn't nice! Oh, and I'll make sure she gets plenty of water, 'cause I know how 'portant it is—for a dog to drink plenty of water, I mean.''

Lily repressed a giggle; she couldn't have Nate thinking she wasn't taking him seriously. ''I'm sure you'd make a wonderful master,'' she said again, ''but—''

''Who do you think you are,'' a deep male voice interrupted, ''making decisions regarding my son without discussing them with me first?''

Blinking, Lily sat in stunned silence for a second. ''Max, I—''

''If and when Nate gets a dog, *I'll* be the one who gives the go-ahead, not you!''

''I—I never intended to—''

''How do you expect me to deal with his disappointment, now that you've got his hopes up that he'll get a dog?''

''Max, if you'll just calm down for a minute, I can explai—''

"There's nothing to explain. Your 'find the mutt a home' scheme may have worked in the past, but it isn't going to work this time."

It was pretty obvious by the tone of his voice, by the heat in his words, that Max had no intention of listening to reason. She didn't understand the level of his anger. Especially with little Nate within earshot.

As Lily saw it, she had two choices: sit quietly as Max continued his tirade, or hang up.

If she hung up, Nate wouldn't have a chance in a million of adopting Missy. But if she stayed on the line, maybe she could slip a word in edgewise…if she was patient until Max spent the last of his wrath. *Lord,* she prayed, *give me the strength to know when to speak…and what to say when I do.*

"I've had it up to *here,*" Max was saying, "with people who think they know better than I what's good for my boy. Especially people like you, who don't even have kids of their own!"

That hurt, Lily admitted silently. And it was unfair, to boot. Because she might have kids of her own, if loving Max hadn't made every man look so sad by comparison.

"Stick to what you know, Lily—animals. And let me raise my son in peace."

He seemed to have run out of steam. In the moment of silence that followed his last stinging remark, Lily debated whether or not to stand up for Nate. The boy clearly wanted—and as Georgia had pointed out, *needed*—something to occupy his lonely hours. Seemed to Lily he needed something to love, too—

something that would love him in return, unconditionally.

"Are you finished?" she asked.

He cleared his throat. "Yes."

"May I have a moment, then, to explain?"

"There's nothing to explain," he shot back. "I'm—"

"I'm sure you don't *mean* to sound like an unreasonable bully, but…" She paused.

She listened to the silence and prayed he hadn't hung up. Then he coughed, and she added, "If you'll just be quiet for a minute, I'll be happy to tell you what's *really* going on here."

"Go on," Max said, his voice tight.

She sighed heavily. "Nate called just now to—"

"*He* called *you?*"

"Yes, he did, to thank me for rescuing Missy at—"

"I heard all about it on the news. 'Lily, the hero of Texas wildlife.'"

Lily ignored his caustic tone and continued. "He called to tell me he'd overheard Georgia and me talking earlier, in the diner. I'd stopped by to ask her if she'd mind having a dog underfoot…*if* you gave Nate permission to have a dog, that is." Not the whole truth, but not exactly a lie, either. But what was she to do, faced with his irrational ire? It didn't seem fair for Nate to suffer because his father was a loud-mouthed know-it-all! "Mind you, I'm no expert when it comes to what's good for kids, but it isn't Nate's fault that he jumped to conclusions based on the small portion of the conversation he overheard, because, after all—'' she narrowed her eyes and accentuated each word ''—he's *only...four...years...old!*''

This time, Lily didn't much care if he hung up or not. Then again, if he actually was the stodgy old grouch he'd sounded like, he might make Nate pay for the scolding she'd just given him.

''Max,'' she began, tempering her voice, ''I know it's been a long time since you've spent any time in my company.'' Long time, she laughed to herself. What a joke! Max *never* had spent any time in her company, because he'd always preferred short-skirted cheerleader and prom-queen types—a far cry from what Lily had been—and from what she'd become! ''But you need to know, I would never do anything so underhanded as to get Nate's hopes up about getting a dog—not without making sure it was okay with you first.'' This time, thankfully, the whole truth and nothing but.

When he didn't respond, she added, ''So here's the lowdown. The dog is a golden retriever, one of the gentlest breeds God created. She's smart, well-trained and quiet. She'd make an excellent companion for Nate. Georgia says there's room for her in the apartment. I'm sorry the little guy overheard the conversation, but now that the cat's out of the bag, the ball's in your court.'' Lily groaned inwardly at the back-to-back clichés. ''Think about it for a couple of days. I'll hold off finding a home for Missy 'til I hear from you.''

And with that, she banged the receiver into its cradle.

''Take *that,* you bossy, swaggering—!''

"My, what was *that* all about!"

Lily turned toward the sound of the friendly voice. "Hey, Cammi." She slumped onto the nearest hay bale. Immediately, Missy curled up at her feet. "That was Max."

"Uh-oh," her older sister said. "I'd heard he was back in town, but I was hoping you could avoid a collision."

Lily only shrugged.

"So tell me, how's he look?" She wiggled her eyebrows and winked. "Handsome as ever?"

"Yeah, I guess."

Cammi ruffled Missy's thick golden fur. "Still stuck on the big galoot, eh?"

"Yeah, I guess," she said again.

"Didn't sound much like it when I walked in."

Lily filled Cammi in on what had happened, from their sister Violet's call to her hanging up on Max.

"Wow. Somebody put some starch into your spine, I think. Never thought I'd see the day you'd stand up to him, not knowing how you've always felt, anyway."

Cammi was the only person on earth who knew that Lily loved Max—that she'd loved him when she was twelve and he eighteen, that nothing had changed, not a whit, in the years since. She sighed.

"You really ought to see other guys," Cammi suggested. "Who knows? Maybe God has put your Mr. Right out there someplace, and He's just waiting for you two to bump into one another." She sat beside Lily, draped an arm over her shoulder. "How you gonna find your knight on a white steed if you never leave this barn?"

"I'm content, right here, doing what I do."

"Baloney. You were born to be a wife and mother. This—" Cammi waved a hand, indicating the cages and the critters in them "—this *stuff* you do is proof you're filled to overflowing with natural nurturing tendencies." She held up both hands to stall Lily's retort. "You're doing great work here, nobody could quibble with that. But be honest with yourself, kiddo. Wouldn't you rather be spending all that love and care on children of your own? On a husband?"

Yes, Lily thought. But only if Max were her husband and the father of those children.

"Well, I didn't come here to lecture you, so how 'bout we talk about the reason I *did* come?"

Lily forced a grin. "The wedding?"

"Yup. Did you get your dress yet?"

On a sigh, she said, "No. Not yet."

Cammi frowned. "What's the matter? You don't like the style?"

"It's fine. Gorgeous, in fact. We'll all look like fashion models. It's just…I haven't had time."

Her sister stood, put both hands on her hips. "You have three weeks to pick up that dress and have it altered. It isn't like you have a choice. You're the maid of honor, don't forget. How can I get married without you there by my side?"

Lily got to her feet and hugged Cammi. "I know. I'm sorry. You have enough on your mind with all the last-minute plans. I'll do it first thing tomorrow. I promise." She brightened to add, "Did you get all the presents put away yet?"

Cammi groaned. "Not yet. There were about a hundred women crowded into the living room. Must have taken you weeks to get the shower organized."

"Took longer to recuperate, once it was over!"

The sisters laughed, and Missy barked happily.

"Tell you what, since tomorrow's Saturday, how 'bout when you pick up the dress, we meet for lunch," Cammi suggested. "My treat. Least I can do for you throwing the biggest, bestest shower a bride ever had."

"It's a date."

"Let's meet at Georgia's. I have a ton of stuff to do in town, anyway."

Georgia's? And risk seeing Max there?

"If he's there," Cammi said knowingly, "we'll talk loud and fast about the new love of your life." She giggled and crouched to hug Missy's neck. "He doesn't have to know it's a dog!"

"Maybe I ought to borrow that sweater," she said, grinning as she plucked a shiny dog hair from Cammi's shoulder. "He'd think my new beau was a blond!" Lily walked her sister to the door. "On second thought, it would be a waste of perfectly good playacting. Max doesn't care who I see. Truth is, that scolding he gave me earlier was the most attention he's paid me, ever."

"Then, we'll do something better than try to make him jealous."

"What's that?"

"We'll ignore him." Cammi headed for the house. "See you at supper, kiddo?"

Smiling, Lily nodded. "Sure."

Ignore Max Sheridan? It would take more than a wedge of lasagna to give her the strength to accomplish a feat like that!

Chapter Three

"Lily?"

She recognized the dee-jay-type voice immediately: Max. Just what Lily needed—a run-in with him on the telephone just before bedtime. "Yes," she said cautiously.

"Sorry to call so late, but I wanted to wait until Nate was asleep."

Why, she asked silently, *so he won't get upset when you start browbeating me again?* "What can I do for you?"

Missy padded up, circled several times, and flopped at Lily's feet. She patted the dog's head as Max sighed heavily into her ear.

"I don't blame you for being mad. In fact, that's one of the reasons I'm calling…to apologize. I had no right chewing you out the way I did this afternoon. Especially since I didn't have all the facts. Nate and my mother explained things, and, well, I'm sorry."

"It's okay. I understand." She didn't, but if saying so made his apology easier...

"Do you? Understand, I mean?"

"You've got a lot on your mind these days, what with your mom needing surgery and all."

"Frankly, Mom's leg was the last thing on my mind when we spoke earlier. I just..."

She could picture him, running one hand through his hair and staring at the ceiling, the way he had as a teenager, when nervousness or frustration got the better of him.

"Max, really," she said, feeling an unexplainable need to rescue him, "it's okay. Water under the bridge." She frowned, wondering why she'd been speaking in clichés lately. Maybe, Lily thought, because the wisdom of each adage "fit" better than brand-new ideas?

"You don't have to go easy on me. I can take it on the chin. Especially when I deserve it." He hesitated. "And I deserve it."

She heard the smile in his voice, and grinned herself. "Okay then, next time I see you, I'll give you a good whack and we'll call it even."

Max chuckled. "You always were a good-natured little thing."

Always were? Meaning, he'd noticed something about her back then? Lily didn't quite know what to make of that. She'd always suspected he only saw her as incidental, as someone who stood on the fringes, as a girl who was never a real part of things. To find out he'd seen her, that he'd watched and listened closely enough to know she was good-natured...

She knew her heart had better quit beating double-time or it would jump clean out of her chest. "So, how did things go with Nate? Is he terribly disappointed?"

"Why would he be disappointed?"

Lily rolled her eyes. *Oh, no reason,* she thought, *except, maybe, that Nate wants a dog, and because his dad thinks he's master of the universe and wasn't properly consulted, the answer is no.* "Well, you're not going to let him have Missy, right?"

At the mention of her name, the retriever raised her head and met Lily's eyes. Funny how quickly the pup had adapted to her new moniker. If Lily were the type to read meaning into every little thing…

"Not necessarily. I explained to him that a dog is a big responsibility, especially one like Missy, who'd need regular brushing, *especially for a kid who's only four.* Besides, she hasn't been lost for more than a few hours. Her owners might claim her in the next day or two and…"

Lily didn't hear anything Max said after "owners." She'd put a half-baked effort into finding out who Missy belonged to, tacking Lost Dog posters on a few telephone poles, mentioning during the TV interviews that she'd keep the pup until it could be reunited with its family. But there was more she could have done, like running ads in the local papers, placing announcements on the radio. Lily had done it all so many times that "getting the word out" had become second nature.

So, why not this time?

"Nate understands we'll consider taking Missy—

and I stressed the word *consider*—*only* if her owners can't be found.'' He paused. ''How long does that usually take?''

Lily snapped back to attention. ''If she fell off a boat, as the rangers suspect, it shouldn't take long at all. In fact, I'm surprised she hasn't been claimed already.'' It was true, after all. If Missy had been her dog, she'd have been frantic with worry. Which raised the question: If the dog *had* fallen from a boat, where was the boat?

''Well, I won't keep you. I just wanted you to know I didn't mean to come off sounding like—what was that you called me?—a bully.'' He chuckled. ''You always did have a way with words.''

And there it was again—''always.''

''If I'd used that tone on the job, maybe I wouldn't have had so much trouble collecting fees from my clients!'' he said.

Georgia had told Lily that Max had earned his CPA, then worked his way up the corporate ladder to a partnership at one of Chicago's most prestigious accounting firms.

He laughed again. ''I can be a blockhead sometimes. I'll just thank my lucky stars you're the forgiving sort.''

Lucky stars? This, from the boy who used to depend on the Lord's help by praying before every game, who sang solos in the church choir, who regularly talked his peers out of smoking and drinking because it wasn't the behavior of believers?

Georgia had said something else, too: Max had lost his faith after his wife's suicide.

"You are the forgiving sort, aren't you?"

"Sure," she said, "'course I am."

"Whew. All that silence made me think maybe you were looking through your phone book for the nearest knee cracker."

"Knee cracker?"

"You know, guys who take baseball bats and teach people—" He cleared his throat. "Never mind. Long as you're okay."

For the second time, Lily felt an overpowering need to reassure him. "It'd take more than a brow-beating from you to do me any lasting harm." So far, that was the biggest whopper she'd told, because his reprimand had hurt her, far worse than it should have. "Guess it's only natural you'd assume the 'daddy' role," she added, grinning, "seeing as you're so much older than I am."

"You sure know how to hurt a guy. Guess I don't have to wait to see you to 'take it on the chin,' do I!"

Odd. He sounded serious. But how could that be, when she'd intended her remark as a joking reminder. Since Lily always tagged along with her older sisters and their friends, she'd frequently been their I-told-you-so target. Once, when a particularly humiliating comment put tears in her eyes, Max had slung an arm over her shoulders. "Aw, don't take 'em seriously," he'd said. "They don't mean anything by it. They're just practicing for when they're parents themselves one day."

"But I'm almost thirteen," she'd cried, "not *that* much younger than the rest of you!"

She remembered the peculiar look that had crossed his face. "Six years," he'd said, his voice trembling slightly as he withdrew his arm. "More than enough to make a guy—"

A cheerleader ran up and hugged him just then, preventing him from finishing the sentence. It was such a common occurrence—girls throwing themselves at him—that Lily didn't give it another thought. Until now.

"I'm not *that* much younger than you," she said, returning to their present conversation. Hopefully, he'd remember the scene from their past, too, and finish his sentence this time.

"Well, guess I'll let you go. I promised Mom I'd open the diner in the morning. Five o'clock rolls around faster than I'd like to admit."

"You slept late when you were a corporate big shot, eh?" she teased.

"Not really. Most days, I was up by six, out of the house by seven. Until—" He cleared his throat. "Slept later once it was my job to get Nate ready for the sitter."

Which used to be his wife's job, Lily surmised.

"So, you'll be on duty at lunchtime?"

"Yeah," Max said. "Why?"

"Cammi and I are meeting at the diner at noon." She told him about having to pick up her maid of honor dress and get it altered for Cammi's upcoming wedding—a stall tactic, because hadn't Max said he'd called for *two* reasons?

"Cool. Guess I'll see you then, then."

How long since she'd heard him say "then, then"?

Lily wondered. *Too long.* And she'd missed it. Missed everything about him, from that way he had of bobbing his head when listening to others, to the way he looked deep into a person's eyes when he was the one doing the talking. She missed the delight he seemed to get from little things, like helping someone by picking up a dropped book or holding open a door. If schoolmates seemed down in the dumps, his antics were sure to raise their spirits. And then there were the adorable dimples that formed beside his sexy half grin.

"Yeah." *I'll see you then, then,* she added silently.

"If you're lucky, I'll pay for your dessert."

If she was truly lucky, he'd pay her a little one-on-one attention!

"What was the other thing you called about?"

"Other thing?"

"You said..." She didn't want to remind him of the apology; in her opinion, his discomfort had caused him to squirm long enough. "Never mind," she said, hoping the disappointment didn't ring too loudly in her voice. "I'll see you tomorrow."

"Who was that?" her dad asked when she hung up the phone.

"Max Sheridan." And now that she had a moment to think about it, had he been flirting with that "pay for dessert" comment? *Don't be silly, Lily.*

"Sherman Tank Sheridan?" Lamont whistled. "Man, could that boy throw a pass! If the Cowboys could get a couple guys like that on the team..." Her dad went silent and met Lily's eyes. "What's he doing calling you?"

The flirtation question died a quick death when she realized her dad was right; why would the handsome, former star quarterback be interested in Lily London? She bent to kiss her father good-night. Still, it sure sounded like Max had been flirting.

Lily couldn't concentrate on an answer. Not while looking at her father's puzzled expression. "Bacon and eggs in the morning?" she asked, heading for the stairs.

"Mmm," he grunted, flapping his newspaper. "Girls," he muttered. "Never could understand 'em."

It wasn't the first time she'd heard him say that. And with four daughters born in quick succession, he'd likely say it 'til he drew his last breath.

Maybe someday she'd tell her father what had come to mind every time he'd said it:

Boys are just as confusing!

"I understand congratulations are in order," Max said, when Cammi joined her sister in the booth. "When's the big day?"

"Three weeks from today. If I'd known you'd be in town, I would have sent you an invitation."

As they chatted, Lily sat back, smiling and thinking that Cammi had been looking particularly beautiful these days. She'd always been one of the prettiest girls in town, but since Reid had come along, she practically glowed. *Thank you, Lord,* she prayed, *for sending him into her life.* What were the chances He'd send a man like that into Lily's life?

Cammi dug around in her purse, pulled out an invitation. "This came in today's mail. One of Dad's friends can't make it." She handed the tiny envelope to Max. "Why don't you come in their place, and bring your little boy!"

Lily's heart thumped so hard, she thought surely anyone in earshot could hear it. *Don't take it, Max,* she prayed. *Don't take it.* She didn't want him there. Because Cammi had hired a band to play forties music, and he'd always loved to dance. Lily didn't want to watch him move across the floor with another woman in his arms!

"Your mom already RSVP'd," Cammi was saying, "so I'll rearrange the tables so the three of you can sit together."

Max tucked the invitation into his shirt pocket. "Thanks. Maybe Nate'll meet some kids his own age, 'cause it looks like we'll be staying in Amarillo longer than we thought."

Cammi frowned. "I heard about your mom's leg. What a shame." She brightened to add, "But she's on every prayer list in Texas, so she'll come out of it better than new." As an aside, she said, "Besides, the way I hear it, her surgeon has more reason than most to succeed."

Max's expression darkened, and Lily wondered if it was because he didn't approve of his mom's relationship with her doctor, or because Cammi had mentioned prayer. The latter, probably, she decided, remembering what Georgia had said about his faith crisis.

"I didn't pack a suit for Nate, but we have three weeks to buy—"

"He doesn't need a suit," Lily cut in. "He's four years old. No one's going to notice if he's not dressed up like a tuxedo advertisement."

Cammi pointed. "Oh, Max, is that li'l cutie over there Nate?"

He looked over his shoulder to where his son sat, deep in concentration as he colored on construction paper, and nodded. Lily couldn't help but notice how his entire demeanor changed at the mere sight of the boy. He stood taller and smiled. Not that half-baked grin he'd been tossing around since he'd come home, but a genuine, full-faced, two-dimpled smile. If anyone doubted Max's love for Nate, they need only see him now to believe how much his son meant to him.

Lily frowned. "He looks a little pale today. I hope he isn't coming down with something."

Max's wide grin faded. "His appetite has been off the past week or so. And he isn't sleeping well, either."

"Probably just having trouble adjusting to the climate," Cammi offered. "The Texas Panhandle is very different from Illinois."

"Yeah, maybe." But Max didn't seem convinced, as evidenced by his worried expression. He faced them suddenly and whipped out his order tablet. "So, what can I get you ladies?"

"What, no waitress today?" Lily asked, grinning.

"Flat tire or something," he said. "So I'm 'it' until she gets here."

Cammi was on her feet in no time. "You handle the cash register," she told him, tying an apron around her waist. "I remember from our high school days what happens when someone puts a food-laden tray in *your* hands.'' Closing her eyes, she looked at the ceiling. ''Anyone wearing a white shirt when you walked by was in trouble!''

A quiet *thump* captured everyone's attention.

A woman got to her feet, knocking her plate on the floor when she did. ''This little boy just fell out of his booth!'' she shouted, pointing.

Max was beside his son in a heartbeat. ''Nate?'' He gave the semiconscious boy a gentle shake. ''Nate, what's wrong?''

Lily stood behind him, one hand on his shoulder. Nate's brown eyes looked even darker in his ashen face. Hearing his long, ragged breaths, she said, ''We need to get him to the hospital, now.'' She gave Max's shoulder a squeeze. ''I'll bring my car around and meet you out front in a minute.''

Max's worried eyes met hers briefly before he turned his attention back to Nate.

Lily grabbed her purse from the table and raced for the door, dialing her cell phone as she went.

''Don't you worry,'' Cammi told Max. ''Andy and I will handle things here.'' She met the cook's eyes. ''Right, Andy?''

''You bet,'' he said with a jerk of his spatula.

Cammi held open the diner's door while Max hurried to Lily's waiting car. ''I've already called ahead,'' she said, buckling the seat belt over him and Nate. ''They'll have someone waiting at the E.R. entrance.''

''Thanks,'' he said, as she got behind the wheel.

It didn't escape her notice that there were tears in his eyes when he said it.

Tires squealing, she pealed away from the curb.

Lily glanced at Max, who held his son close. Worry creased his handsome brow and made his jaw muscles bulge as he stared through the windshield. She reached across the seat to pat his hand. "Don't worry," she said. "Everything will be fine. He's in the Lord's capable hands."

Max grunted, then pressed a kiss to Nate's temple.

Pay him no mind, Lord, she prayed. *He's just had a rough go of things lately.* But even as the thought formed, Lily knew better; Max had been nursing his grudge against the Almighty for a long, long time. But she didn't have to worry. The God she had come to know had a great capacity for love, infinite patience, boundless mercy; He wouldn't hold Max's anger against him.

Now, if only she could convince Max of that.

"Don't worry, Mrs. Sheridan," the nurse said, "your little boy is in good hands. Dr. Prentice is the best pediatric cardiologist in the area."

Lily started to correct the woman. "I'm not—"

"Thanks," Max said, sliding an arm around her waist. "That's good to know." And once the nurse left Nate's E.R. cubicle, he added, "We can set her straight once Nate's out of harm's way. Right now, I'd rather she put her full concentration on doing her job."

Lily nodded, feeling an odd mix of confusion and gratitude. For years, she'd dreamed of being Mrs.

Maxwell Sheridan...but this wasn't the way she'd pictured it happening.

Dr. Prentice blasted through the pastel-striped curtains, clipboard in one hand, stethoscope in the other. "So who do we have here?" he said, wiggling Nate's toes. He draped his stethoscope around his shoulders and slid a pair of black-framed half-glasses from his lab coat pocket. "Says here your name is Nathan," he said, squinting at the chart. "Okay if I call you Nate?"

Smiling feebly, the boy nodded.

Dr. Prentice balanced the glasses atop his balding dome. "Well, Nate, we're gonna run a few tests, see what put you in here. And once we find out, we'll do everything we can to make sure it never happens again. Whaddaya say to that?"

The smile broadened slightly as Nate gave another nod.

The doctor faced Max, held out a hand. "I see you've already signed the necessary consent forms, so there's no reason to keep him waiting." He winked at Nate. "We'll get you home fast as we can, okay?" Waving Lily and Max nearer, he perched on the corner of the gurney and addressed his comments to Nate. "Here's what we're gonna do: First, we're gonna show you all sorts of neat machines. X-ray, electrocardiogram, echocardiogram. Nate, m'boy, you're gonna feel like you're the star of a science-fiction movie!" He wiggled the boy's toes again. "Now, I know you've seen all this stuff on TV, so I really don't need to tell you that not one of these tests is gonna hurt, not even a little bit—right?"

A look of wide-eyed fascination brightened Nate's pale face.

"After we're finished with the big gizmos, we'll do a couple of blood tests. Ever stick yourself with a pin, kiddo?"

"Yessir. And once, when my dad and me were fishing, I got a fishhook stuck in my thumb." He showed the doctor a tiny crescent-shaped scar.

"Man," Dr. Prentice said. "How'd you ever get the hook out?"

"Dad cut the sharp part off with pliers."

"Wow. Bet you cried buckets."

"I didn't cry at all, did I, Dad."

Max grabbed Nate's hand. "Not a single tear. You were tough as nails."

"I'm impressed," the surgeon said. "And that run-in with the fishhook? I can absolutely guarantee the blood tests won't hurt *nearly* as much! Just a teeny tiny pinprick, one for each test. You think you can handle that?"

Nate lifted his chin. "Sure. No sweat," he said, grinning to prove his bravery.

"Well, we might as well get busy, then. Sooner we get started, sooner you can go home." He stuck his head out into the hall and summoned a tall, lanky orderly. "George, drive my friend Nate here to the X-ray department, will ya?"

"Can…can my dad come, too?"

Hearing the tremor in Nate's voice, Lily grabbed his hand, gave it a gentle squeeze. He squeezed back.

"The more the merrier," Dr. Prentice said. With

that, he strode from the cubicle, white lab coat flapping behind him.

"Gotta oil these wheels," George said as the gurney squeaked down the hall. "Sounds like somebody ridin' over and over a mouse's tail, don't it!"

Nate grinned. "Yeah. A mouse's tail." He giggled softly.

"You'll like Doc Prentice. He's the best."

When Lily let go of Nate so George could steer the gurney into the elevator, Max grabbed her hand. "Thanks," he whispered.

"For what?" she whispered back.

He only shrugged. "Just…thanks." And as his son had done moments before, Max squeezed her hand.

She wanted Max to be happy, the way he was back in high school. Wanted Nate to be safe and healthy, too. Lily stared at the toes of her white sneakers. *Everything's going to be all right,* she said to herself. *The Lord will see to it. He makes miracles happen every day, right?*

But she knew only too well, having lost her mother when she was barely Nate's age, that not every story has a miracle ending. She closed her eyes tight. *If anyone needs to witness a miracle, Lord,* she prayed, *it's Max.*

"I know I neglected to tell Nate about the catheterization earlier, but I honestly didn't think we'd need one. The test results make it necessary." Dr. Prentice leaned against a wall in the small waiting room as Max and Lily sat woodenly on orange and blue upholstered chairs.

"Sounds painful," Max said.

"I won't lie to you...it's not comfortable. But I'll give him a local anesthetic, and a mild sedative, as well. He'll be loose as a goose by the time we do the procedure—probably be asleep through the whole test."

Lily leaned forward. "Will we be able to stay with him the whole time?"

"I don't have a problem with that, long as you don't mind gowning and masking up." The doctor pulled a chair around to face them and sat down. "That kid is a real trouper, all right." A look of genuine admiration crossed his face. "He's seen half a dozen technicians this afternoon alone, who introduced him to some weird-lookin' gizmos. Most kids don't come through it the way Nate did. He's brave, that boy of yours."

Lily bit her lower lip, wondering if now was the time to 'fess up, admit she wasn't Nate's mother. Max slid an arm behind her, as he had in the E.R. cubicle.

"He's truly a gift from God," she said instead.

The words were no sooner out than Max withdrew, sat forward and leaned both elbows on his knees. "How'd this happen?" he asked. "I mean, what caused Nate's fainting spell?"

"Well, I won't know for sure until all the rest of the test results are in," Dr. Prentice said, mimicking Max's pose, "but from everything I've seen so far, it looks to me like he has an atrial septal defect...a hole in his heart."

Max swallowed so hard that Lily heard it from where she sat.

"A hole in his heart? Why hasn't he shown symptoms before now?"

"I wish I had some concrete answers for you, Mr. Sheridan, but the fact is, we don't know for sure. Some kids are born with it. In other cases, a bacterial or viral infection is the cause. The thing to remember is, we can usually repair things, and most kids grow up to live perfectly normal lives."

Max hung his head. "Should I have known? I mean…" He ran both hands through his hair. "If I'd been on the ball, would I have noticed something, and maybe headed this off?"

"Absolutely not. Kids get fevers and colds, and most of the time, the stuff clears up and goes away. Other times, some damage gets done. There's no reason to beat yourself up because there's absolutely no way you could have predicted this."

Dr. Prentice faced Lily. "I must say, Mrs. Sheridan, you're awfully calm and quiet." He smiled. "Now I see where your boy gets his stoicism. Can I answer any questions about your boy?"

"Much as I wish it were true, Nate isn't my boy," she blurted. "I'm just a friend of the family."

"Not *just* a friend," Max put in. "I don't know what we'd have done without you today."

The doctor continued his explanation. "The catheterization isn't as gruesome as it sounds. We'll insert a small plastic tube in through Nate's groin, moving it slowly until it reaches his heart. Then we'll take some blood samples and measure blood pressure through the catheter. We'll inject some blue fluid through the tube into a blood vessel in his heart. The fancy word for the process is *angiocardiography*. But in plain language, it's an X-ray that'll let us see what's wrong with Nate's li'l ticker.''

''How long will it take?'' Lily asked.

''Oh, an hour, maybe two, usually.''

''And how long before we can talk to him?''

''Takes a few hours for the sedative to wear off. He might wake up with a slight fever, an upset stomach, so don't be concerned. That'll all pass in a couple of hours, too. And by that time, I should have the rest of the test results back, and we can talk about treatment.''

''Treatment?'' Max's voice was thick with emotion.

''Could be we'll find it's not a large enough hole to require anything further. Or, he might just need surgery. But let's not put the cart ahead of the horse, okay?'' He grabbed one of Max's wrists with his right hand, one of Lily's with his left. ''No sense getting all worried and upset until there's a good reason for it. And I see no reason for it at this juncture.''

Max inhaled a deep breath and held it, while Lily rubbed soothing circles on his back. Dr. Prentice got to his feet. ''Get some rest,'' the doctor said. ''Hopefully, you won't need it.''

But his ''just in case'' warning was clear, all the same.

He walked backward down the hall, talking as he went. ''See you bright and early. I've scheduled the procedure for 8:00 a.m.'' He saluted, then rounded a corner and disappeared.

Lily and Max sat in stunned silence. "You want to get back to Nate?" she finally asked.

"Yeah," he said, nodding. "Poor kid's probably wondering what's going on." He turned to face her. "You don't have to stay. I know you have a ton of stuff to do, what with your animals and all."

She didn't want to leave him, not for a minute, not even for her beloved animals. And from the look on his face, Max didn't want her to go, either.

Lily rested a hand on his forearm. "Cammi has helped out more times than I can count. She knows what needs to be done."

He rubbed his eyes. "You sure? 'Cause I can hitch a ride with—"

She flipped open her cell phone. "I'll only be a minute."

He stood slowly. "Thanks. You're—"

"—dialing Cammi. Now go," she said, shooing him with her free hand.

Max grabbed her fingertips, pulled her into a one-armed hug. "Aw, Lily, why can't life be simple?" He breathed into her hair. When he stepped back, there were tears in his eyes. He swiped at them, then shook his head. "Go on. Make your call. I'll meet you in Nate's room."

She watched him walk down the hall, head low, hands pocketed. Her heart ached for him…and throbbed with love for him, as well.

Chapter Four

Lily made the call to Cammi as she headed for the hospital chapel. With her sister's promise to "pinch hit" for as long as need be echoing in her ears, she knelt in the front row and recalled the way Max had looked, sitting in front of Dr. Prentice. Someday, maybe she'd understand what had turned him from happy-go-lucky boy into a serious, no-nonsense man.

"Lord," she prayed, "help me know how to comfort Max. Give me the words to reach him, and guide me in knowing when to speak those words." For now, she'd simply be his friend.

Invigorated by her decision, she hurried back to Nate's room. The four-year-old was sleeping peacefully when she peeked in, so Lily tiptoed inside and stood beside Max. "How's he doing?" she whispered.

"Fine," he said softly, "all things considered."

"Any news from the doctor?"

He shook his head.

She looked at Nate. "Natural sleep, or drug-induced?"

Max pointed at the plastic tubing connected to the bag hanging above Nate's bed. "Sedative. Nurse told me he'd be out most of the night."

"Let's go to the cafeteria, then—get you a sandwich and something to wash it down with." She took his hand. "You haven't had a bite all day."

"How do you know that?"

"Well, have you?"

"I had breakfast...."

His usually strong voice sounded forlorn. "Remember what Dr. Prentice said."

"What?"

"He said you needed to rest because you might need it later."

"Oh, that," Max said. "I'm not tired. Besides, he said *we,* not me."

"Anyone would be tired after six hours in a hospital," she said, tugging his arm. "Especially when you've spent most of them pacing."

When he got to his feet, she added, "Dr. Prentice was right, you know. No matter what those tests tell us, Nate is going to need you at one hundred percent."

He glanced at the boy, whose small chest rose and fell with each soft breath. "He still looks so pale."

Sandwiching Max's hands between her own, Lily forced him to meet her eyes. "You have to believe he'll be fine, have faith that everything will turn out all right!"

She watched as his dark, long-lashed eyes bore into

hers. If she didn't know better, Lily would have said it was love beaming back at her. But, of course, it wasn't, she told herself. Gratitude, maybe. Exhaustion, even. But love? Who was she kidding!

His stomach growled just then, making them both grin.

"I hate to say 'I told you so,' but..." She laughed. "Let's get something into you before you have everyone thinking there's a grizzly bear loose in Pediatrics."

A sad smile was his answer. He looked at Nate again. "I don't want to leave him. What if he wakes up?"

She could have hugged him right then. "Okay, I'll go to the cafeteria, bring you a sandwich and a soft drink." Lily headed for the door. "Or would you prefer coffee?"

"Doesn't matter." Then he said, "Thanks, Lily."

"You're beginning to sound like a broken record," she teased. "Really, there's nothing to thank me for. What are friends for, after all!"

He slouched back into the chair beside his sleeping son's bed. "You're way past being a friend. Way past."

How *far* past friend? she wondered as she walked toward the elevator. Dare she hope?

No. Especially not now. Max was worried, confused. It simply wasn't fair to expect him to talk rationally under such stressful circumstances. Wasn't fair to expect him to talk about *anything* but his son. Maybe when all this ended and Nate was home again, safe and sound, *then* she'd hope. Maybe. Meanwhile, she'd support Max in any way possible, do anything for him she could.

How could she help him most right now?

First, by getting some nourishment into him, and when he'd had his fill, she'd suggest a much-needed nap. And while he slept, she'd pray.

The image of Nate, melting to the floor at Georgia's, flashed in her mind. No flu bug had caused his collapse.

Yes, she'd pray, because she had a feeling Max was going to need all the God-given strength he could get these next few days.

Max alternated between pacing the gray-tiled waiting room floor and fidgeting in the itchy upholstered chairs. Lily, on the other hand, sat beside him, calm and quiet, leafing through her Bible.

He found it hard to believe she'd brought the thing along. Did she always carry it with her? Well, he was glad if she found comfort in its gilt-edged pages. Hadn't been so long ago he found solace there himself. No, it had been years ago, before life taught him that consolation—what little the world had to offer— came by dint of his own determination and the sweat of his own brow.

He leaned back in the chair, one leg bent at the knee, the other stretched out in front of him. This waiting would drive him nuts, if Lily hadn't decided to stay with him. He peeked over at her, watched how intently she focused on God's Word. Maybe she'd be spared the hard lessons that had taught him prayer was an exercise in futility.

It hadn't saved his dad, who'd devoted himself to the church and spent every spare moment in prayer, hadn't saved his brother, who'd joined the seminary, intent on becoming a missionary—and died when the Africa-bound plane crashed. Didn't protect Georgia from being widowed at a young age, though she'd devoted her life to the church.

And it hadn't saved his marriage.

Max leaned his head against the wall and closed his eyes. If he believed in prayer, he'd say one now, to silence the memories whispering at the corners of his mind.

Long before she'd started to threaten suicide, and had been under psychiatric care for her depression, Melissa had tested the limits of his patience, spending more than they could afford, disappearing for days on end, then bringing unwholesome types home with her. They had no place else to stay, she'd insist. "We can't call ourselves Christians if we turn our backs on the needy!"

The "needy" kept her too busy to cook or do laundry. If any cleaning got done around the house, it was Max who did it—after a long, hard day at the office. Mostly, he took it on the chin and prayed for patience...until Nate was born. Then he prayed motherhood would change her.

It did not.

His prayer life ended that awful evening when he came home from work and found her, lounging on the family room sofa with her latest needy person...while Nate stood crying in his playpen, soiled diaper hanging loose from his pudgy body and a bent cigarette in his dimpled hand.

Max prayed for forbearance as he cleaned tobacco bits from his son's weeping face and chubby fingers. Prayed for strength as he tucked the baby into his crib. Prayed for self-control, so he wouldn't do more than boot her latest long-haired friend out of the house.

As he tossed the man's guitar case and duffel bag onto the lawn, Melissa said, "You've embarrassed and humiliated me for the last time, Max Sheridan." She tossed the musician's rumpled T-shirts and tattered jeans into a brown paper bag. "If I can't even choose my own friends, then tell me, what do I have to live for!" Tucking the sack under her arm, she stormed out of the house.

Max flung open the door and followed her onto the porch. "What about Nate?" he'd called after her. "You leaving him, too?"

She had turned halfway down the walk to face him. "Yes, I guess I am."

She'd made him angry before in their five-year marriage, a hundred times, but never like that. "You don't deserve a kid as great as Nate."

"Maybe not, but he's stuck with me, thanks to your insistence that we make a baby!"

White-hot rage burned in him as she climbed into the front seat of her ruddy-faced visitor's pickup. "Maybe you're right, Melissa. Maybe you *don't* have anything to live for." Then he'd slammed the front door so hard that the impact cracked both narrow windows beside it.

Always before, prayer had helped him find the

strength to tolerate her erratic behavior—to forgive it, even. Not that night! He hoped that in the morning, he'd find it in himself to forgive her, yet again, for her indiscretions, for neglecting Nate, for disrespecting *him*.

The baby fell asleep in the queen-size bed, sucking his thumb and cuddled in the crook of his daddy's arm. When the sun woke Max the following morning, he laid Nate in his crib, then padded on black-socked feet to the kitchen to brew a pot of coffee.

He'd decided halfway through his fitful near-sleepless night that first thing in the morning, he'd find a full-time sitter for Nate. Melissa had proven once and for all that she couldn't be trusted to care for him. And while Max waited for the coffee to perk, he'd make a few calls. Plenty of folks at his office enrolled their kids in day care; surely one would have an opening.

But he never made a single phone call, never started that pot of coffee, because the instant he'd set foot on the cool white tiles, he saw Melissa...slumped in a ladder-back chair, long, tangled blond hair splayed across the tabletop. "What're you doin' *this*—"

The next five or ten seconds seemed like hours.

First, he saw the note, crumpled beside her right hand. The pen with which she'd written lay on the floor near the fridge, its cap half hidden under the dishwasher. "You're right," Melissa had scribbled on the back of an overdue bill, "I have nothing to live for. Please don't teach Nate to hate me." She'd underlined *please* three times, and hadn't bothered to sign her name.

The amber-colored pill bottle lay open and empty beside the note, its white cap tucked in her left hand. She was breathing, but just barely, so he'd grabbed the phone and—

"Max."

Someone was shaking his shoulder. A soft voice said, "Max? You're white as a sheet."

He looked into big green eyes. Eyes that shimmered with worried tears. Eyes fringed by thick black lashes. Beautiful eyes. Loving eyes. *Lily's eyes.* For that moment, at least, his upside-down world was right side up again.

Then Max remembered where he was, and why.

His heart thumped and his pulse pounded. If anything happened to that kid…

"Max," Lily repeated, a hand on either side of his face. "You're shaking like a leaf. What's wrong? Talk to me or I'm going to start hollering for a doctor."

She gave his face a gentle shake, much as he'd shaken Melissa that night. The way he'd shaken Nate on the floor of the diner. If anything happened to that kid…

"Shouldn't be hard to find one. We're in a hospital, you know."

He blanketed her hands with his. "Sorry. Didn't mean to scare you." But he knew that he had; fear was written all over her face. All over her pretty, loving face.

She knelt on the floor in front of his chair and

grabbed his wrists. "What on earth were you thinking about just now? You were a million miles away. Why, if I believed in ghosts, I'd say you saw one just now!"

He had, in a way…but Max couldn't tell Lily that, now, could he? At least, not without admitting he believed he felt partly responsible for Melissa's suicide. He'd never said as much, not to anyone, and sure couldn't confess the awful truth to Lily! Not here. Not now, with Nate going through who knows what in the O.R.

"I'm told I'm a pretty good listener," she said, smiling softly.

He'd known since she was a knobby-kneed sixth grader and he was a junior at Centennial High that Lily London had a crush on him. But because they were separated by six years—an important six years—Max never allowed her to face it. Hadn't faced it himself…until today.

He kept telling himself that someday, she'd grow up, find a man who'd love her as she deserved to be loved. Then Max would become a dim memory and she'd wonder why she'd wasted so many years dogging his heels, waiting, hoping.

She'd grown up, all right. But she hadn't found her Mr. Right. Because she was still waiting, and hoping? "Your heart is as big as your head," he said, chucking her chin.

Lily laughed. "My, but you do know how to turn a girl's head, don't you?"

He tucked a dark curl behind her ear. He'd always wondered what her hair might feel like. It was shinier than his mother's favorite satin bathrobe. He imagined it would be softer than the mink stole his grandma wore. And he'd been right. His fingers seemed to have a mind of their own as they combed through her luxurious waves.

Long, lush lashes dusted her cheeks as she pressed a light kiss to the heel of his hand. "Don't worry, Max. You're going to be all right," she whispered. "And so is Nate."

He drew her closer, his thumbs tracing slow circles on the smooth contour of her jaw. "You're sure of that, are you?"

When she nodded, a curl fell across one eye. At that moment, she didn't look anything like the freckle-faced girl she'd been. Lily was a full-grown woman, and the six years between them didn't mean diddly anymore.

"Yeah," she sighed. "I'm sure."

His forefinger drew the outline of her full, pink lips. Lips that had spoken kind, comforting words. Lips that had smiled reassuringly. Sweet lips...

Max stood, pulled her to her feet and kissed her.

She returned it, he couldn't help but notice. Wrapped her arms around him and held on as if finally, at long last, she had what she'd waited her lifetime for. If only he could tell her it's what *he'd* wanted, too.

Guilt surged through him at the admission. He'd married Melissa because he couldn't have Lily. She'd been too young, he'd been too impatient. Too impatient to wait until she was old enough.

So he'd leaped into a full-blown relationship.

With the wrong woman.

For all the wrong reasons.

Melissa was dead now, in part because he hadn't been the husband he should have been. Oh, he'd tried to love her, had tried to build a life with her, raise a family. But the ugly truth was, he'd done it all…to forget Lily.

Marrying Melissa had been a mistake. A terrible, tragic mistake. One he'd regret—and pay for—the rest of his days.

His son lay unconscious in the next room, with a hole in his little heart. Would the surgeon be able to repair it? Or would Nate continue to weaken?

Lily snuggled closer still, blurring the lines where she ended and he began. He ended the comforting kiss but didn't let her go. Couldn't let her go…not just yet. She felt good in his arms, so good, pressed close to his heart. It felt right, holding her, kissing her, and yet…

So much time had passed since he'd left for Chicago, yet nothing had changed.

He still yearned for Lily, and she still deserved better than the likes of him.

"Nate will be fine," she said again, leaning her cheek against his chest. "You'll see."

She'd misread his mood, he realized. Big-hearted, see-the-good-in-everyone Lily had convinced herself that the entire cause of his misery was concern for his son. Well, there was more to it! It was also about believing Lily would never be part of his life.

Max kissed the top of her head and heaved a sad

sigh. "I hope so." *Hard to believe a man could mess up his life as badly as you have in just thirty years.*

"And *you'll* be all right, too."

Maybe. But he sure didn't deserve to be all right. Physically healthy, yes, because Nate needed him, more now than ever. But emotionally? Nah. He didn't deserve that, not one whit.

"Thirsty?" she asked.

He wasn't, but nodded anyway.

"You stay here, in case Dr. Prentice comes out to talk to you about Nate. I'll find a vending machine, get us something cold to drink."

He nodded again. My, but she was beautiful, especially looking up at him that way, her enormous green eyes brimming and shimmering with full-out affection. She looked at Nate that way, too—proof she'd be a loving, devoted mother. If only…

No point torturing yourself, he thought. Dreams like that were for schoolgirls, not grown men who'd botched up their lives.

"Back in a jiff," Lily said, popping a tiny kiss to his chin. "Don't pace a path in the floor while I'm gone, okay?" she called over her shoulder.

He smiled despite himself. *And don't you be gone too long,* he thought. Because if Dr. Prentice came through the O.R. doors and the news wasn't good, well, Max knew he couldn't face it without her standing beside him. He didn't want to face anything, not even *good* news, without her beside him!

Max watched her walk down the hall. When she disappeared around the corner, he flopped onto a tweedy-seated waiting room chair and knuckled his eyes. "Shouldn't have kissed her, Sheridan. Should've kept your big dumb lips to yourself."

Because now that he knew it was everything he'd dreamed it would be, he was a goner. Her helpful nature, her nurturing tendencies, her adorable gestures—they'd all plucked a chord in him that he hadn't even known existed, putting music and harmony and balance into his dreary, lonely life. But that kiss…

She deserved better, and if only she'd give herself half a chance, Lily could find happiness with another man.

Another man? The mere thought made his heart ache, made his stomach lurch, made his ears hot. The picture of her, smiling that *smile* of hers for some other guy, kissing some other guy the way she'd just kissed him…

Max drove his fingers through his hair. Why was the stupid procedure Dr. Prentice was giving Nate taking so *long?*

On his feet again, he walked the length of the hall and back again. All right, so Lily would marry someday, have a couple of kids, live the rest of her days fulfilled and satisfied and, yes, happy. And he'd make himself be happy *for* her.

Because, to put it simply, she deserved it…and he didn't.

"What we're going to have to do," Dr. Prentice said, tugging off his surgical mask, "is called a keyhole bypass." He sat across from Max and leaned his elbows on his knees. "I've done dozens of 'em, and it's usually the last step in cases like Nate's. Minimally invasive—doesn't require me to crack the sternum.''

Max nodded while Lily patted his hand. If only she could do something to fix everything wrong in his life! That power, she knew, was God's and God's alone, and she prayed that when this was over, Max's faith in the Almighty would be back, and stronger than ever.

Dr. Prentice, meanwhile, grabbed one of the paper napkins she'd brought back from the cafeteria. Clicking his ballpoint pen, he began drawing a diagram of the human heart.

''See, Nate has a hole, here, in the top chamber of his heart, called a secundum atrial septal defect. Fortunately, there's an adequate rim around the hole to allow us to implant a device to close it.''

Prentice scribbled, while Lily watched Max trying to take it all in.

''My team and I are gonna close that hole up,'' the doctor continued, ''using an Amplatzer occlusion device. Basically, it's nothing but a wire mesh disk that's about the size of a dime.''

''How long will it last?'' Max asked.

''It's made of nickel and titanium, and filled with polyester fabric, so I'd have to say forever. In a few months, it'll be completely covered by heart tissue, which means it'll be a permanent part of Nate's heart wall.''

Max put the drawing down and hung his head.

''Sounds scarier than it is,'' Dr. Prentice said.

''So, how does it work, exactly?''

"We'll insert it into a catheter that we'll run through the femoral vein in Nate's groin to his heart. When the disk comes out the other end, it'll deploy—open up kind of like a tiny umbrella against the inner and outer walls of the heart, directly over the hole."

"Sounds dangerous," Max said, staring at the drawing. "What are the risks?"

Dr. Prentice shrugged one shoulder. "The whole process is far less formidable than open-heart surgery. But it's surgery, nonetheless, which means there's a small chance of bleeding, infection, perforation of the heart, device embolization—"

"Embolization?" Max picked up the napkin, turned it this way and that.

"An obstruction, like with a blood clot. But that's rare, very rare. Once we get the thing in place, we'll watch for leaks, and—"

"Leaks?" Max's head snapped up.

"Again," Dr. Prentice stressed, hands up to forestall Max's fears, "that's the exception rather than the rule. Couple months back, I performed the procedure on a little girl with a condition similar to Nate's. Took less than two hours, and she was sitting up in bed, playing with her little brothers soon after the anesthesia wore off—and home again the next morning."

Relief softened Max's features. "How's she doing now?"

Prentice winked. "According to her mom, she's running the pants off her brothers."

"Will he be in much pain?"

"For the first few days he might experience some slight discomfort, but that'll pass quickly."

"Will he be able to feel it?" Max winced. "I mean, when he moves around, will it—"

"Not one of my patients has indicated they're aware of its presence at all."

"So he'll be a normal, active kid again afterward?"

The doctor laughed. "I didn't have a chance to spend much time with Nate, but it didn't take long to figure out he's the kind of kid who isn't gonna let anything slow him down much." He stood, patted Max's shoulder, then headed back to the O.R. "He'll be fishing and swimming and chasing down pop-flies in no time. Don't worry," he said over his shoulder.

"Easy for you to say," Max muttered as the doctor left. "Nate's not your son."

Lily stood beside him, leaned her head on his shoulder. "Easy, now. He'll take good care of Nate. The nurses say he's the best in Texas, and I say he's a good man."

He brought her into the circle of his arms. "I understand how his reputation as a surgeon precedes him, but you just met him. How could you possibly know what kind of man he is?"

"I looked into his eyes," she said, blinking up at him. "And you know the old saying…"

One side of Max's mouth lifted in a wry grin. "Well, if he slips up, even a little—" he shook his fist "—I'm gonna shatter both of those windows to his soul."

Lily giggled and wrapped her hands around his fist. "C'mon, tough guy. Let's go see your kid."

The next days passed in a flurry, with Lily staying at Georgia's apartment with Nate while Max waited outside the O.R. during Georgia's leg surgery. Lily fully expected that once his son and mother were home again, Max would relax.

But he didn't.

After interviewing a dozen nurses, he hired a pleasant, middle-aged woman to look after Georgia and Nate while he worked in the diner. And he worked from dawn 'til dark, filling in wherever he saw the need—bussing tables, washing dishes, mopping floors. When he wasn't busy with patrons and staff, he pored over the ledger books in the cramped, cluttered office space behind the kitchen.

If she didn't know better, Lily would have said he was intentionally avoiding any contact with people—herself in particular. Because every time she'd called to ask how his mom and little boy were progressing, he'd answered with one-word replies. The first few times, she blamed his tone on stress, but by the sixth or seventh call, Lily felt she had no choice but to assume Max didn't want to talk to her.

His attitude answered her *unasked* questions, too, things she'd been asking herself ever since that wonderful moment when Max had tenderly held her close: What had his breathtaking kiss *meant?* Was it proof he cared for her, too? Dare she hope their relationship could begin to shift, gradually, from friendship to…more? Or had it been simply the result of Max's mounting worries about his little boy's condition. Had she mistaken his reaching out to her for comfort and reassurance for blossoming love?

Lily decided she wouldn't make a fool of herself,

not even for Max Sheridan, not even if she'd loved him since junior high. She'd always been close to Georgia, and almost from the instant he burst into the diner, Lily had adored little Nate. Max's chilly conduct couldn't change that. So she'd call when he was working in the diner, ask the nurse to put Georgia on the phone, find out what she needed to know about Georgia and Nate without the grumpy, distant middleman!

She'd done well with her new "be cool" attitude, balancing the ranch checkbook and caring for her winged and furred charges with visits to Georgia and Nate, real well. Until the church social.

How Georgia managed to get Max to attend was anybody's guess. But there he stood in the food line, filling a plate for Georgia, another for Nate. She knew neither plate was his; Max had never liked chicken wings, and a healthy portion of the golden-fried stuff lay on the foam dish. Blue jeans clung to his muscular thighs, and he'd rolled back the cuffs of his white shirt, exposing brawny, slightly hairy forearms. He'd gotten a haircut; she knew because when he'd kissed her outside the O.R. that day, her fingers had played in the dark waves caressing the back of his neck....

Stop it! Lily scolded herself. Remembering that moment, and how it left her weak-kneed and dizzy, accomplished nothing. Well, that wasn't exactly true—memories of that sweet slice of time made her yearn for him all the more, because she'd so wanted to believe it meant as much to him as it had meant to her.

"Hey, Snow White!" Georgia hollered from across the room.

Smiling, Lily crossed the green-tiled floor of the church basement and grabbed a chair. "Nice to see you're getting around without that wheeled contraption of yours," she said, kissing the redhead's cheek.

"Couple more weeks of physical therapy," she said, thumping the rubber-tipped end of her cane on the floor, "and I'll be rid of this, too!"

"I imagine you're chompin' at the bit to get back to work."

"Are you kidding? I've loved every minute away from that greasy spoon of mine." She looked around, waved Lily closer. "I'll let you in on a little secret, if you promise to keep it to yourself."

Nodding, Lily pulled an imaginary zipper shut across her mouth. "Mmmm's the wrrrd," she said through tight lips.

One last scan of the room told Georgia no one else could hear. "Robert asked me to marry him," she whispered.

Lily's eyes widened as she leaned back and gasped. "That's wonderful news! Why do you want to keep it a secret?"

"He hasn't told his kids yet, and I haven't had a chance to tell Max and Nate, either."

Lily frowned. "You don't look very happy about it. Don't tell me you said no."

Georgia made an are-you-kidding face and said, "Don't be ridiculous! He's a wonderful, loving man. I'd be crazy to let him slip through my fingers."

"Then, why the long face?"

"I have another bit of news, and I'm not too sure Max is gonna like it."

Lily giggled nervously. "You're not pregnant, are you?"

Georgia laughed. "'Course not, you silly nut!" When the moment passed, she said, "I'm going to retire. Permanently. Robert, too. We're going to take a world cruise for our honeymoon."

"Why would Max object to that? You've worked hard in that diner all your life."

"Because I want to hand the deed to that diner over to him. It's been in the family for generations. I don't want it going to strangers."

Lily thought about that. He'd pulled hundreds of shifts in the diner as a boy, and although she'd never heard him complain, exactly, if his expression and body language were any indicator, he hadn't liked the work one bit.

And he'd spent the past six years in the big city, no doubt working at a big fancy desk in an air-conditioned, mahogany-paneled office. Probably lived in a ritzy Chicago suburb, too, in a too-big-for-him house on a street with other snooty accountants.

"What scheme are you two cooking up?"

Lily lurched and Georgia gasped.

"Oh!" Georgia exclaimed. "You just shaved ten years off my life, sneaking up on us that way!"

Max chuckled. "I didn't sneak. It's just that you two were so deep in discussion, you didn't hear me." He raised an eyebrow. "So, what gives?"

"None of your beeswax, boy," Georgia said, chin

in the air. "Honestly, how old does a mother have to be to get a little privacy?" She sniffed.

Max held up his hands in mock surrender. "*Excuse* me for interrupting. I only came over to deliver your plate." He put the dish on the table, then handed her a paper napkin and plastic utensils.

"Kids," she said to Lily, "never get too old to lay a guilt trip on you." Rolling her eyes, she sighed. "Sorry for snapping your head off, son."

"Yeah," he said, laughing, "*that* sounded sincere!"

"Where's Nate?" she asked, changing the subject.

He pointed. "Over there, with the pastor's kids. He's lovin' it here."

Georgia nodded. "It's good to see him so happy."

"And healthy," Lily put in.

He looked at her then, as if seeing her for the first time. "Right," he agreed, smiling sheepishly. Pocketing both hands, he said, "So, how have you been?"

"Fine." She squirmed on her chair. "You?"

Max nodded, lips pressed tightly together. "Fine. Fine."

"You look a little tired," she admitted, "here, around the eyes."

He ran a hand through his hair. "Nah. It's eyestrain. I've been getting Mom's books in order." Max shot Georgia a feigned stern glance. "It's been a while since she balanced the checkbook."

"Honestly," she huffed, "do you have to air *all* my bad habits?"

The three of them grinned nervously for a moment before Max broke the silence. "Lemonade, ladies?"

"None for me, thanks," Lily said, standing. She didn't know how much longer she could remain this close to him without crying. Because, like it or not, she loved him still; admitting he didn't feel the same way—and never would—hurt. Cut deep. Time healed all wounds, as the sages promised, but Lily had a feeling she needed distance every bit as much as she needed time. She headed for the card table that held bottles of soda, lemonade and iced tea. "Take it easy, Georgia," she said, waving.

"Wait," Max said, grabbing her elbow when he caught up with her. "What's your hurry?"

Lily lifted her chin a notch. "I'm not in a hurry. I just saw—" she picked someone out of the crowd at random "—Cammi over there. I forgot to ask her something earlier."

"Really?" he said, a suspicious smile on his face. "What?"

Pursing her lips, she said, "Something to do with the wedding. Girl stuff." He hadn't let go of her elbow, she noticed; the warmth of his big hand spread all the way to her fingertips. He stood so close she could inhale the crisp manly scent of his aftershave. She missed him desperately, though they'd never been anything but friends. But that didn't stop her from wanting more, from dreaming and praying for more. Knowing she'd never have it was enough to break her heart.

Lord, she prayed, *save me or I'll fall apart right here in front of him!*

Lily tugged free of his grasp and hurried to where Cammi stood, arm in arm with her fiancé.

"Hey, kiddo," Reid said when she walked up. "What's wrong?"

"Nothing," she snapped. "What makes you ask a question like that?"

"Oh, I don't know," her future brother-in-law replied. "Maybe that 'I just lost my best friend' look on your face?"

She'd never been a crybaby, had never been one to give in to tears. For a reason she couldn't explain, Lily felt a sob aching in her throat. It wasn't likely she'd actually *cry,* but just in case, before the dam burst, she ran to the ladies' room.

"What did I say?" she heard Reid ask Cammi.

"I'll find out what's wrong," her sister said as the door swung shut.

Lily locked herself in a stall and pressed her forehead to the cool, pink-metal wall. What was *wrong* with her? She'd had years to get used to the idea that Max would never be part of her future. Nothing had changed, so why the tears?

"Lily? Are you okay in there?"

She nodded, and then, realizing Cammi couldn't see it, said, "Yeah. I'm okay."

"You want to talk about it?"

She shook her head. "No. Not really."

"It's about Max, isn't it. I saw you two talking earlier. You want me to sic Reid on him? He can fix it so the lout wears black eyes and a swollen lip for weeks."

Lily snickered. "Thanks, but I'd hate for Reid's fingers to be too swollen next week to wear his wedding band." She opened the stall door and stepped into the comforting circle of her sister's open arms. "Oh, Cammi," she sighed, biting back tears. "What's wrong with me?"

Cammi held her at arm's length. "Not a thing. It's *Max* who has the problem."

She wrinkled her forehead. "Max? But—"

"He could have the sweetest, prettiest girl in Texas for his own, if he'd just open up his eyes and see what's right in front of his face."

"His very handsome face," Lily said, grinning.

"Okay, so he's cute. I'll give him that much." Cammi walked to the sink, jerked a brown paper towel from the dispenser. "But he isn't as smart as I thought he was." She dampened the towel, then pressed it to Lily's cheeks. "He's got some silly notion that life is a ledger book where everything is black and white."

She took the towel, dried her eyes with a corner of it. "I don't get it."

"You don't fit nice and neat in a column, and until he can find a way to make things between you add up…"

Lily gave a deep sigh. "You're giving me a headache," she teased. "You know I never was any good at math."

Cammi laughed and draped an arm over her sister's shoulder. "Yeah, right. The gal who has kept dad's ranch running for a decade, all by herself, isn't good at math."

"That's different. It's—"

"Black and white. I know." She opened the door and led Lily back into the church hall. "Look around you, kiddo," she said, a bent forefinger guiding Lily's chin. "There are other fish in the sea, as they say." She kissed her sister's cheek. "Your problem is, you have an aversion to worms. Can't bait the ol' hook if—"

Lily laughed. "I feel that headache coming on again."

"Well, if you're okay, I'm going to get a slice of peach pie for Reid, before it's all gone. It's his favorite, you know."

Nodding, Lily winked. "I'm fine. Go 'do' for your man." She gave her a playful shove. She had no idea what kind of pie Max preferred, or whether he preferred it to cake, or how he voted in the last election, or if he liked classical music. She didn't know his favorite color, or if he wore glasses to watch TV. She knew he liked fishing, but only because she'd overheard Nate telling Dr. Prentice about the fishhook in his thumb.

So what are you blubbering about? Lily asked herself. It seemed ridiculous, getting all teary-eyed and heartbroken over a guy she knew so little about, a guy who barely had given her the time of day. The concept brightened her mood.

Until she saw him, laughing at something Reid had said. She might not know if peach was his favorite pie, but she knew this:

She loved him. Always had.

And always would.

Chapter Five

Lily sat at the head table, pretending to enjoy the filet mignon and caramelized potatoes on the gold-rimmed china dinner plate in front of her. Lamont had gone all out, a string quartet playing "The Wedding March" in the church balcony, biggest banquet hall in the hotel, Amarillo's best chef. Everything looked wonderful, right down to the fluted vases where colorful Japanese fighting fish swam in the center of each table. The bride looked like a fantasy princess in her designer gown and veil, and the groom, her storybook prince.

If happiness could be measured by looks alone, the newly married Mr. and Mrs. Reid Alexander would live in bliss from this day forth. Lily knew the union would be rock solid, forever, and not because of gauzy veils, satin-lapeled tuxedos and thousands of white roses. Cammi and her new husband had been the perfect love match, from the moment they crashed into one another outside of Georgia's Diner. Why perfect? For starters, both loved the Lord with all their hearts.

Lily wanted a love like that—a marriage like her sister's would surely be. She sighed and sipped ice water from a crystal goblet. Fat chance of that happening if she couldn't get over this thing for Max Sheridan. She'd been compiling a "Reasons It Won't Work Out" list, and at the very top, wrote, "'Yoke ye not to unbelievers....'"

Had Cammi deliberately seated Max so that he faced the head table? Or had it been a ridiculous coincidence? She tried not to look at him, at his dark, shiny curls—her image of male perfection in his tidy gray suit and bloodred tie, smiling as he cut his son's steak into bite-size pieces. He loved that kid more than anything in his life, and it showed. Didn't he realize Nate had been God's greatest gift to him? That alone should give him more than enough reason to believe!

The photographer dashed past, blocking her view of the Sheridan table. She watched the balding, pot-bellied fellow hurry from table to table, leaning and crouching and kneeling, cameras clicking as he captured guests laughing, dancing, waving and shouting to friends across the banquet hall. The waitstaff bustled in and out, delivering coffee, hustling dirty dishes into the kitchen. The maître d' pointed the way to the rest rooms as the bandleader announced the title of the next song.

Controlled chaos, Lily thought, grinning wryly. The scene reminded her of a wedding she'd attended last summer. Cammi had scowled at the groom's drunken uncle. ''When *I* get married,'' she'd steamed, ''there had better not be anything like that frozen on film in *my* wedding album!''

The photographer snapped Lily's picture just then, startling her so badly that she actually said ''Eek!'' Who said that, she wondered, besides cartoon mice! She blinked past the blue dots floating before her eyes, feeling suddenly self-conscious. Hopefully, when that picture was developed, it wouldn't upset Cammi.

Lily wasn't accustomed to wearing her hair this way. Every time she'd tried an updo, unruly wisps escaped, no matter how carefully she secured them. Squinting into the bowl of a sterling soupspoon, she tucked in a wayward curl and checked her lipstick. *Well, you won't win any beauty contests,* she thought, putting the spoon beside her plate, *but hopefully, you won't make anyone lose their lunch, either.* Smiling at her little joke, Lily glanced up…directly into Max's smiling brown eyes.

He'd caught her primping! And his teasing, all-knowing expression told her he'd lumped her in with every other prissy, vain female he'd ever met. Lily groaned inwardly. She'd been watching him from the corner of her eye all during the meal. Why had he picked *that* moment to look up! If only he would take the time to get to know her, he'd realize that fussing with her hair and makeup had never been high on her priority list.

Forcing a grin, Lily returned Max's snappy little salute and turned to the groomsman seated beside her. ''Would you mind passing the salt, please?'' she said, though nothing on her plate needed salting. Really, what did it matter *what* Max Sheridan thought of her, she fumed, absently thanking the tuxedoed gent when he handed her the shaker. It wasn't as though Max's opinion of her would enhance their relationship, such as it was.

She forced herself to focus on the conversation at the opposite end of the head table: "We've had such unseasonably icy weather for November," said a bridesmaid. "Plays right into my plans to go skiing over the Thanksgiving holiday," said another. "Do you have a bandage?" the skier asked. "These newly dyed shoes gave me a blister the size of my nose!" Better to listen to the chitchat than admit that there *was* no relationship between her and Max…and that there likely never would be.

It took all the willpower she could muster to avoid looking toward his table. She knew he was watching her; it seemed his big dark eyes were boring holes into the side of her head. But why would he watch *her,* when at least a dozen eligible bachelorettes had come to the wedding, sans beaus?

"May I have this dance?"

Lily looked into the grizzled face of Hank Gardner, one of her brother-in-law's ranch hands. It was no secret the man was sweet on her; he'd made sure she knew, every chance he got.

"Oh, go on," Cammi insisted, giving Lily's shoulder a gentle nudge. She leaned in close to whisper, "Guess who is watching. Give him an eyeful!"

The sound of butter knives clinking against water goblets interrupted the sisters' secret conversation.

"Ah," Cammi sighed, feigning boredom, "a woman's work is never done." Then she faced her new husband and gave her guests exactly what they'd asked for.

Hank pulled out Lily's chair. "C'mon, Lil," he said, grinning good-naturedly, "song's half over already!"

Lily let him lead her to the dance floor, where the band was playing an old Patti Page ballad.

"You look gorgeous," he said, taking her in his arms. "Don't tell anybody, but I think you're prettier than the bride."

"When was the last time you had your eyes checked?" she teased. Leaning back slightly, she wiggled the knot of his silk tie. "I must say, you clean up real good yourself!"

Hank blushed. "Had to borrow it from Reid. Must be eatin' too many biscuits with supper, 'cause the shirt collar's a mite snug." He looked into her eyes as the female singer crooned.

"Nice song," he said.

"Very nice." Lily had hummed it dozens of times when trying to soothe an injured animal. "It's one of my favorites—"

"May I cut in?"

Hank's brows knitted in the center of his forehead. "I reckon." But it was obvious to anyone within earshot that he wasn't any too happy to hand over his dance partner. The cowboy stepped away but held tightly to Lily's hand. "Be gentle with her, bud," he told Max, "'cause this purty li'l gal is a genuine blue-ribbon prize."

Nodding, Max stepped into Hank's place. "He's right, you know," he said once the cowboy had walked away.

How would you know? she wondered. Max didn't know her well enough to testify to that.

"You're the most beautiful woman in the room, bar none."

Lily felt her face go hot. Heart hammering, she wanted to protest, because in the first place, Cammi was the bride, and in the second...

She was quoting him, Lily realized, with her "first" this and "second" that. Absurd, especially considering how little time she'd spent with him. "You look nice, too." But the compliment paled against the truth. Max truly *was* the best-looking guy in the room.

She couldn't seem to get her mind off the warmth of his hand, pressed gently against her lower back as he guided her across the parquet tiles. That, and the way the fingers of his other hand linked almost possessively with hers.

"Nate looks adorable," she said, mostly to distract herself. "How's he doing?"

"Pretty well, all things considered." He paused, touched her chin with a bent forefinger. "I've never seen you with your hair up before. Looks gorgeous. Very sophisticated."

She grinned self-consciously. "You've seen it up, plenty of times. Ponytails, braids—remember?"

He pulled her a little closer, ran a fingertip down the bridge of her nose. *"This,"* Max whispered, his nose a mere fraction of an inch from hers, "is not the girl I remember at all. *This*," he said, bringing her closer still, "is all woman."

Lily licked her lips and swallowed. If she didn't know better, she'd say Max was gearing up to kiss her—right here in the middle of the crowded dance floor, with her father and sisters and the pastor watching.

"Don't worry," he said on a chuckle. "You're safe. There's a time and a place for everything."

How could he have known what she'd been thinking? Nothing was making sense, especially considering the way he'd snubbed her these past weeks. What kind of head game was he playing? she asked herself. She ought to walk away, leave him standing there alone.

The song ended, and she admitted she'd never have done anything of the kind. He brushed her cheek with a gentle kiss. "Thanks for the dance," he whispered into her ear. "It was a real treat."

She grinned as he headed back to his table.

Strange how, throughout the remainder of the reception, Max managed to find her, no matter what maid of honor duties she was performing. He was there when the best man gave a long-winded toast to the bride and groom. During the father-daughter dance, he surprised her by sliding an arm around her waist. He stood shoulder to shoulder with her, watching as Cammi and Reid cut the wedding cake. And when she joined the unmarried females to compete for the bridal bouquet, Max caught her eye from the other side of the dance floor.

She'd only stepped into line to be a good sport...

and because the photographer literally dragged her there. Lily had no intention of reaching up, of actually trying to catch the flowers. It was a silly superstition, a fun tradition, nothing more.

Was she seeing things, or had Max mouthed *Good luck!* from his side of the floor? Lily never had time to answer, because on the bandleader's count of three, she reached up without even thinking…and caught the bouquet in one hand.

When her gaze met Max's, he winked, gave her two thumbs up. It would be interesting to see the wedding album a week or two from now. Would the photograph of her catching the bouquet show a starry-eyed young woman in love…or the look of stunned disbelief she truly felt?

No time to answer that question, either, for it was time to help the bride change into her going-away outfit. Lily had packed her sister's suitcase, making sure to include the lovely white nightgown a neighbor had given Cammi at the bridal shower.

How long before her dad and their longtime neighbor Nadine would announce *their* plans to wed? Lily wondered as she unfastened dozens of tiny satin-covered buttons on the back of Cammi's dress. Had she been the only one who'd noticed the way they'd sat all through the reception, staring lovingly into one another's eyes?

She considered the question as the dwindling number of wedding guests gathered in the lobby of Amarillo's Grand Hotel to say goodbye to Cammi and Reid. First thing in the morning, the couple would board a Florida-bound jetliner that would take them to Miami, and from there, they'd cruise the Caribbean. While the band packed up and the last well-wishers finished up the remaining hors d'oeuvres and pastries, Lily began loading beautifully wrapped presents onto a wheeled cart.

A commotion in the lobby captured her attention. Lily ran toward the hotel's main entrance and stood on tiptoe to see what all the ruckus was about. When she spotted Max on all fours beside his unconscious son, Lily elbowed through the crowd and knelt beside him.

"What happened?"

"Dunno," he muttered. "He just…collapsed."

She put a hand on his shoulder. "Where's your cell phone?"

Hands trembling, he gave it to her. She flipped it open. "Is Dr. Prentice's number programmed into this thing?"

"No. Uh, I think so. Yeah, under *P*."

When the phone's highlighter bar illuminated the doctor's name, she pressed "Send" and got to her feet. "Don't you worry, Max," she said, grabbing her car keys from the tiny purse that matched her gown. "Meet me out front." She held up two fingers. "Two minutes. I'll call ahead to the E.R., tell them to expect us."

Bolting across the parking lot, Lily thanked God that the hospital was only a few blocks from the hotel. "Lord," she said, revving the motor, "get us there fast, and watch over little Nate in the meantime."

She pictured the boy's face…so much paler than when he'd fainted in his grandmother's diner weeks ago. Something was wrong, terribly wrong. Had the patch Dr. Prentice placed over the hole in Nate's heart come loose? The surgeon had said it could happen. Extremely unlikely, but possible.

She parked beside the curb, ran around to the passenger's side and flung open the door. Max held Nate close as he climbed into the bucket seat.

And hadn't Dr. Prentice said Nate could bleed to death if that should happen? Lily tried to look confident and smiled bravely as she clicked the seat belt into place across them.

"We really have to stop meeting this way," he said as she slid behind the steering wheel.

Despite his half grin, she could see that Max was terrified, far more afraid this time than he'd been when they made their last trip to the E.R.

No surprise, Lily thought, because Max had heard Dr. Prentice's warning, too.

"Sorry, Mr. Sheridan, but you're not a compatible donor."

Max looked grim as the doctor added, "It's fairly common—a parent having a different blood type than his child."

"Spare me the lesson in hematology, Doc. Just tell me what you're gonna do to save my son."

Dr. Prentice took a deep breath, as if summoning patience. "We're searching the blood bank now. Hard to find AB negative, and that multi-car pileup on the Interstate cost us our last unit of O positive. We've put the word out that we need donations. Might take a couple hours."

"He could *bleed* to death in a couple hours!" Max shouted. Hands fisted beside him, he said, "Where's the nearest supply? I'll drive there myself and get it, bring it back here!"

"Max," Lily said, laying a hand on his forearm, "I'm O positive. I'll give Nate whatever he needs."

He looked at her, blinking as if she'd spoken in a foreign language. "You…you'd do that?"

How could he even ask such a question! "Of course I will." She faced Prentice. "What's the procedure? You have to draw some blood, test it—then what?"

The doctor patted her biceps and then headed down the hall. "Right this way," he said, ushering her into an E.R. cubicle. "I'll have a nurse get you started."

Lily was about to follow the surgeon when Max grabbed her hand. "I…I don't know how to thank you."

"Have faith, Max—faith that everything is going to be all right," she said, meaning it. "That'll be thanks enough for me."

Max was young when his father died—barely sixteen.

His dad had taught him how to parallel park, safely merge and change lanes on the Baltimore Beltway, but didn't live to see his son get his driver's license.

He'd taught Max how to catch a pop-up fly ball, how to keep score during a football game, how to bait a fishing hook. But there'd been countless other lessons he'd learned at his father's knee, too. To defend himself against the schoolyard bully…without becoming one himself. To behave like a gentleman, even if the girl he was with hadn't earned it. To do his level best, no matter how menial or trivial the task.

And the most important lesson of all—to stand up to the responsibilities and obligations that went hand in hand with being a man.

He wanted to teach Nate those lessons, wanted to show his boy, by example, as his father had taught him, the fruits of hard work and determination.

Would he get that chance?

Or would *God,* in His so-called infinite wisdom, decide to take Nate, as He'd taken Max's father, his brother, and in a roundabout way, Melissa.

Icy fear pricked at his soul, chilled him to the bone. Max shivered unconsciously. The very thought of losing Nate made his heart beat like a parade drum, made his pulse pound like a jackhammer.

He'd gladly gone to work every day, built a house in a safe Chicago suburb, where his kid could attend the best schools the state could offer. To accomplish all that, he'd had to give up his reckless bachelor ways—no more skydiving, no more river rafting. It hadn't been a sacrifice. Quite the opposite! Max quickly adapted to fatherhood, and happily looked forward to every moment with his sweet-tempered little boy.

They'd developed quite a bond, Max and his boy.

To lose that now, to lose it *ever*…

Hands linked behind his back, Max paced the hallway outside Nate's E.R. cubicle. *Pull yourself together, Sheridan. You're useless to him this way.* Knuckling his eyes, he took a deep breath, then pushed through the curtains. "Hey, bud," he said, feigning bravery as he kissed his son's forehead. "How you feelin'?"

Nate's sleepy eyes fluttered open. "Better," he rasped, one side of his mouth lifting in a weak grin.

He hated seeing his boy this way—connected to machines and tubes and bags of glucose and medication. If he could lie there in Nate's place, he'd do it in a minute. Had there ever been a time when he'd been this afraid? If there had, Max couldn't remember it.

"In no time at all, you'll be better still." Thanks in no small part to Lily, he admitted.

The boy's lower lip trembled slightly. "I'm scared, Dad."

Max eased his arms under the boy's upper body, hugged him gingerly. "I know, pal, I know." He kissed Nate's temple. "But you're gonna be okay."

"Why does it hurt so bad, Dad?"

Slowly, he released Nate back onto the pillow. "I don't know," he said. "That's what Dr. Prentice wants to find out." He ruffled his son's hair. "Any minute now, he'll take you to the operating room, and before you know it—"

"Will you be in there with me?"

"No, that wouldn't be safe." He winked. "Germs, y'know." He took Nate's hand in his, stroked each small, dimpled finger. "I'll be right outside, I promise."

Dr. Prentice burst into the cubicle and announced, "We'll get that patch put back on your li'l ol' heart in no time, kiddo.'' He pinched Nate's big toe, then added, ''Can I borrow your dad for a minute?''

When the boy nodded, the doctor waved Max outside. He took several steps away from Nate's bed before saying, ''Your girlfriend is a champ.''

Girlfriend. The word echoed in Max's head for a second.

''She's already given a pint of blood, and insisted on staying in there—'' he threw a thumb over his shoulder to indicate the room down the hall ''—until we're sure Nate's out of the woods.''

Max's heart thumped with gratitude…and more. '''Champ' doesn't even begin to describe her.'' Then he added, ''She'll be okay, won't she? I mean, she's barely bigger than a minute herself.''

Dr. Prentice dropped a hand on Max's shoulder. ''Relax. She's petite but strong as an ox.'' He headed toward the O.R. at the opposite end of the hall. ''You can go as far as those stainless-steel doors. There's a nice waiting room right across the way. I'll send a nurse to update you from time to time, and I'll be out to talk to you as soon as we're finished.''

The surgeon had already given Max a detailed explanation of what would happen once those stainless-steel doors closed. If all went well, he'd said, Nate would be in the recovery room in an hour—two, tops.

When he'd learned about the hole in his boy's heart, Max thought the world would surely end; a four-year-old, enduring major surgery! Though the first operation had been a success, he'd always wondered when the other boot would drop, as his mom was so fond of saying. Now it had. "It had better go well this time," he said to himself.

Because if it didn't...

Max couldn't finish the thought. Life without Nate was simply unthinkable.

Lily held the velvety petals of a long-stemmed red rose to her cheek and, smiling, closed her eyes to inhale its delicate fragrance. This latest delivery had arrived shortly after breakfast, and now stood among other gifts she'd received in the week since Nate's operation.

She tucked the flower into the cut-glass vase nestled among shiny brass pots and colorful ceramic containers overflowing with the deep-green leaves of English Ivy, philodendron, and dumb cane blended with assorted mini-palms, and vases of chrysanthemums that filled the window seat in her room. Rooting through empty brown-pleated wrappers in the bottom of the candy box that had come with the roses, she searched for a chocolate-covered cherry. Finding none, Lily settled for a chewy caramel.

Sitting cross-legged on the plush Persian rug blanketing the hardwood floor, she fingered the lovely bracelet glistening on her wrist. A series of *X*s and *O*s, each golden link caught and reflected the sun, flecking the carpet with sparks of amber and shards of bronze.

Every gift arrived by special courier, each messenger bearing a pastel-enveloped card. None of those preprinted verses for Max Sheridan! He preferred the blank-inside kind, so he could spell out his sentiments in strong, bold pen strokes.

Lily read what had accompanied the bracelet: ''Your friendship is more valuable to me than all the gold on earth,'' he'd written. The one that came with the last box of candy said, ''You are sweeter than any candy a confectioner could dream up.'' Asked to choose her favorite, Lily would probably grow dizzy trying to decide!

She called after opening each gift, to thank him, to tell him how unnecessary the gifts were, but always got the answering machine instead of Max. Probably at the hospital, she'd told herself, keeping Nate company. Still, it hadn't been easy, swallowing her disappointment. She missed him, more than she'd imagined it possible to miss another human being.

She thought of the way he'd held her, there in the hospital waiting room, of the way he had eased her into a gentle kiss. Nothing in the thousands of dreams she'd had over the years could begin to compare with the real thing. For the first time since they'd met, Lily felt at peace, felt as though the Lord had heard and answered her prayers. Because surely that loving, tender kiss was proof that Max felt more than mere friendship toward her.

Lily sighed moonily as something drew her back to the card she'd found among crisp sheets of green tissue in the box of roses: ''Red, like the lifesaving blood you shared with Nate.'' Her smile vanished like smoke as hot tears welled in her eyes. Why hadn't she realized it before: The hug, the kiss, every one of these gifts had been inspired by gratitude, and nothing more!

What a fool she'd been, reading more into his actions and his words than he'd intended. Hands trembling, she stuffed the card back into its pink envelope and tossed it onto the pile with other rainbow-hued cards and thanked God that she hadn't been able to reach Max directly. Because wouldn't she look like a silly little twit if she admitted her feelings, and put Max on the spot!

Wiping her eyes with the backs of her hands, she got to her feet and hurried to the barn. She'd encounter no heartbreaking realizations there, no dashed hopes or misguided conceptions. Just the natural appreciation that came when she fed a hungry baby bird or changed a horse's soiled bandage. Her animals didn't expect kindness or generosity. Though some had experienced the pain and horror of neglect or abuse, they'd learned the hard way that disappointment was the other side of the coin.

Over time, she'd taught them that the sound of water bubbling into a stainless-steel bucket meant a fresh drink, that the sight of her big red-plastic grain scoop meant a full feed bag. Wouldn't hurt to take a lesson from *them* for a change, Lily told herself.

Long ago, she'd adopted a strict mind-set, and never allowed herself to deviate from it: Expect the worst; if it happens, you can say 'I told you so!', and if it doesn't, you'll be pleasantly surprised.

Missy trotted beside her from the house to the outbuilding, russet ears keeping time to every paw-beat. Lily crouched beside her, scritch-scratched the thick neck fur. "Starting right now," she said, kissing the bridge of Missy's nose, "we go back to base zero."

First, because Max had more than enough on his mind, with Nate and Georgia so soon out of the hospital, without having to worry or feel guilty about whatever harebrained idea she'd gleaned from his actions.

And second, she was tired of hoping and praying for something that, experience had taught her, simply wasn't going to happen.

Chapter Six

Since donating blood for Nate's surgery, Lily hadn't felt like her usual energetic self. But she'd promised to bake brownies for the church bazaar, and gave the pastor's wife her word to man the "goodies booth" from noon 'til three.

"I'm surprised to see you here," Lily said stiffly.

"Mom wanted to come and she isn't ready to go out on her own just yet." Max put a plate of chocolate chip cookies on the table. "She's plenty ready for baking, though," he said, smiling.

Of course you wouldn't set foot in a church without being forced to! Lily thought. "Where's Nate?"

"Outside, on the playground."

His furrowed brow told Lily she hadn't done a very good job of hiding her feelings. Instinctively, she wanted to ease his discomfort.

"And Georgia?" She glanced around again.

He nodded toward the curtained stage in the church basement, where his mom and her beau sat, holding hands as they chatted with friends. "Robert offered to bring her, but since Nate wanted to come, too, I didn't see any point making the man go out of his way."

"Robert, eh?" She quirked an eyebrow. "Things are pretty cozy between them, I take it."

Max shrugged. "I expect to hear any day now that the ol' boy has popped the question." He punctuated the statement with a ragged sigh.

Frowning, Lily clucked her tongue. "You make it sound like he's about to be escorted to a prison camp!"

"Well, he's been footloose and fancy-free for a couple of decades." Another shrug. "Guess the 'grass is greener' adage fits."

She crossed both arms over her chest. "Oh, really. And why is that?"

"He thinks married life will be better than bachelorhood." Max chuckled bitterly. "I thought so, too…a lifetime ago. If I had an ounce of decency in me, I'd take him aside, tell him some stories that'd make him think twice."

Lily lifted her chin a notch. "If I know your mom, she'll spoil him rotten," she snapped. Just because Max's experience with marriage had been miserable didn't mean every married man would end up miserable. But what did she care about his opinion on husbands and wives and matrimony?

"There's my dad and Nadine," she said, pointing. "Think I'll go over and say hi."

Max wiggled his eyebrows and said from the corner of his mouth, ''Speaking of cozy couples, the pair of them look mighty cozy themselves.''

They did, at that—she had to agree. All right, so maybe they were in love. Last she heard, there was no law against a widower and a widow linking up romantically. Especially when the couple in question had been neighbors for decades…had become close friends after sharing the pain of losing their spouses.

Narrowing her eyes, she glared at him. ''*Some* people believe in happy endings. Just because you have no faith doesn't mean everyone else—''

Brows raised, he held up both hands. ''Whoa,'' he drawled, laughing uneasily, ''easy there, li'l lady. Didn't mean to rile you.'' He looked apprehensive. ''Are you angry with me for some reason? You haven't exactly been your warm, cheery self.''

Shaking her head, Lily looked at the ceiling. She'd promised herself not to behave like a starry-eyed teenybopper if she ever saw Max again…and had intended to avoid him whenever possible. So much for that! But she knew Max didn't deserve to be on the receiving end of her short temper. He had enough to contend with.

Simulating a mischievous grin, Lily said, ''It'd take a lot more than the likes of you to rile me. Sorry if I've been biting your head off. It's just been one of those days.'' Then she winked and spun on her heel and left him standing alone near the enormous stainless-steel coffee urn.

From here on out, she'd have to be a lot more careful, she decided, heading for her dad's table. If Max got wind of her true feelings…

''Hey, cutie,'' Lamont's date said as she patted his shoulder. ''Look who's here!'' Nadine reached for Lily's hand. ''Haven't seen you since Cammi's wedding. My, but you look pretty in that color.''

She'd chosen the ruby-red sheath, hoping it would brighten her mood. It had not. No matter how colorful, clothing couldn't hide the fact that Max's interest was rooted in gratitude and friendship, and that's all it ever would be. She bent to kiss Nadine's cheek. ''How are you?''

She flicked a quick, flirty glance at Lamont. ''Never better.'' Then, blue eyes on Lily, Nadine tucked a blond curl behind her ear. ''And how're *you, darlin'*?''

''Great.'' But she wasn't. Night after night of never-come-true dreams involving Max had made her weary...and brokenhearted. Lily knew exactly what the problem was: she hadn't taken her own good advice and put the matter at the foot of the Cross. Not really, anyway. Starting now, she'd try harder to do just that.

Lily stood behind her dad and patted his shoulders. ''So, what're you two up to?'' she asked, popping a kiss to the top of his gray-haired head.

He turned to face her. ''Up to our Adam's apples in artery-cloggin' food,'' Lamont joked, pointing at his plate. ''Do yourself a favor and grab a slice of Nadine's coconut pie, 'cause it's goin' fast.''

''So much has been going on, I haven't had a chance to ask, how was Abilene?''

Lamont told her about the hearty young bulls he'd bought there, using his hands and animated expressions to highlight the story. He'd always been a hand-some man—tall, broad-shouldered and barrel-chested, with brawny arms and manly hands that belied the thick fringe of dark lashes surrounding his big gray eyes. When he looked at Nadine, those eyes sparkled and he smiled like he meant it. He'd known her since her now-deceased husband had bought the land beside River Valley Ranch, and over the years, they'd be-come friends. It was obvious something else had come from that friendship, and that "something else" made Lamont look much younger than his fifty-five years.

Ten years younger and happier than she'd seen him in decades. *If that's what love can do,* she thought, *maybe Cammi's right.* Maybe she should give up this Max Sheridan dream and find a guy who could return her feelings.

"Oh, by the way," Nadine was saying, "Elmer says hi."

Lily grinned, remembering that a few months ago, she'd nursed the woman's orphaned calf back to health. "I've really enjoyed having him follow me around the ranch, but I hope I didn't ruin him for you like a puppy. He must be huge by now."

"Already twice the size he was when you sent him home. You were wonderful with him, darlin'. I thought sure I'd have to put him down before he mourned himself to death. You're a lifesaver!"

"Lifesaver? I thought her nickname was Snow White," Max chimed in.

When had *he* walked up? And how long had he been standing there?

"Actually, 'lifesaver' *is* more accurate."

Lily tried to ignore the heat in her cheeks, hoped he wouldn't tell them—

"Did she tell you she saved Nate's life?"

Groaning inwardly, Lily held her breath.

Lamont and Nadine exchanged puzzled glances. "I'd heard your boy had a heart problem...." Lamont said to Max.

"But how did Lily save him?" Nadine finished.

"I didn't save him," she insisted. "Dr. Prentice did."

Max harrumphed. "After Nate was out of danger, the doc told me in plain English that if it hadn't been for you, stepping in when you did, he—"

Lily waved his comment away. "Nurses and doctors donate blood all the time. They'd have found someone else."

He shrugged. "Maybe. But none of them was wearing a pretty blue bridesmaid gown—"

"Maid of honor," Nadine corrected with a playful wink.

"None of them was wearing a maid of honor gown, or those pointy-toed, high-heeled matching shoes."

She didn't know what her outfit had to do with anything, but she knew this: Max had an enormous capacity for love and he had proved it that night when he came into the E.R. cubicle to hold her hand while Nate was being prepped for the O.R. He had noticed how cold her hands were and had hunted down a nurse to get a blanket. Such a big heart!

So why couldn't he find room in it for God?

"It was no big deal," she said. "I just happened to be in the right place at the right time."

"Uh-huh." He turned to Lamont and Nadine. "The patch they'd put on Nate's heart had worked its way loose, see, and he was bleeding internally. Hemorrhaging is more like it. I'm not a match, and the hospital had some kind of emergency that made them run out of his blood type." He looked at Lily, a sweet, lopsided grin on his face. "She volunteered to give him as much as he needed, right then and there."

"Doesn't surprise me," Lamont said. "My girl has a heart as big as her head." He sandwiched her hand between his own. "No wonder you've been lookin' a mite pasty-faced these past couple of days. Why didn't you tell me?"

Because you'd have made a big fuss, she thought. "Really, it was no big deal."

"Well, it was a big deal for us," Georgia said.

Lily had barely had time to adjust to Georgia's presence when her boyfriend added, "You're the Sheridan family hero, girl!"

"Dr. Prentice says you saved my life," Nate put in.

Why hadn't she noticed that they'd joined the group?

She'd never been comfortable with compliments, whether about her work, her face and figure, or her so-called good deeds. Lily wanted to bolt from the church basement, go straight home and hide in the barn, where she could do what needed doing and not have to deal with this awkwardness. In their own way, her animals appreciated what she did, too. The difference was, they accepted her nurturing quietly and without question—and didn't embarrass her with a lot of unnecessary thank-yous afterward.

"I'm glad you like the bracelet," Nate said, touching his small forefinger to a golden *X*. "I helped Dad pick it out."

Pride beamed from his big brown eyes, making Lily want to hug him.

So she did.

"I love the bracelet. Haven't taken it off since it was delivered last week." She held him at arm's length to say, "But how did you help your dad pick it out? You were so sick in the hospital!"

"There was a picture of it," the boy said, "in a magazine one of the nurses brought me. I showed it to Dad, and he said, '*X*s for kisses and *O*s for hugs. Perfect for Lily.'"

Lily met Max's eyes. Kisses and hugs. Did he mean…?

He nodded in response, telling her with those big brown eyes of his that Nate might have pointed it out, but *he* wanted her to wear it. Unconsciously, she wrapped her hand around the bracelet, stomach fluttering, her heart clenching. Dare she hope he felt some of what she felt?

Stop it! she scolded herself. *Remember your promise.*

She stood quickly. "Well, I'd really better be going. I haven't fed the animals yet, and I'm sure they're kicking up a fuss."

"The animals? Oh, Lily! Could I come over and

watch you feed them? I won't make any noise or touch anything, I promise. I'll be like a statue.''

To prove it, Nathan stood, stone-still, and stared straight ahead, reminding Lily of the stiff-backed soldiers in the *Nutcracker* ballet. She'd like nothing more, and would have said so, but didn't want to risk a misunderstanding like the one she and Max had had the night she found Missy.

The boy faced his father, folded his hands as if in prayer, and in a soft, sweet voice said, ''Can I, Dad? Please? If you'll take me, you can give me a chore, any chore, and I promise to do it without complaining.''

''C'mon, Max,'' Georgia said, ''take him to Lily's. He'd have a ball!''

''Yes,'' Nadine agreed, rumpling his hair, ''let the kid go, Max.''

Max continued to gaze into Lily's eyes, one corner of his mouth twitching slightly. Lily didn't know if he intended to lash out at the lot of them, as he had that night on the phone, or say yes. She was about to say something along the lines of *This isn't a good time, but maybe another day,* when Max's mouth broadened in a rascally grin.

''Do you have time for gawkers and interlopers?''

Lily looked from his dark eyes to his son's, and sighed. ''No, I don't,'' she began, matching his grin, ''but I have time for you and Nate.'' She had a lifetime, in fact.

Nate jumped up and down, clapping his hands and yelling ''Yippee!'' as Georgia and Nadine made the ''shush'' sign with fingers to their lips.

"I'd say let's all go in my car," Max said. "But how would you get yours home?"

She had opened her mouth to say *Let's meet at the barn,* when Nadine pulled Nate into a grandmotherly hug. "I rode over here with your dad," she told Lily. "Have to go back to River Valley to get my car, anyway, so I can drive your car."

She winked at Lily. Winked! What if Max thought it was a sign that they'd succeeded in pulling off a well-planned plot to get her and Max together?

She chanced a glance at him. If he suspected anything of the kind, it didn't show on his face. He stood, feet shoulder width apart and hands in his pockets, waiting for her to make a decision: drive home in her car, or ride over with him and Nate.

Lily dug her car keys out of her purse, handed them to Nadine. "Thanks, Nadine," she said, hoping she wouldn't regret her choice.

"Only too happy to help out." Another playful wink at Lily before turning back to Lamont. "Well, handsome, you ready to hit the road, or do you want me to fetch you another slab of pie?"

Blushing, Lily's dad grinned and patted his stomach. "Couldn't eat another bite."

"Follow me, then," she said, crooking her finger and wiggling her eyebrows.

Grinning like a schoolboy, he got to his feet. "I'm right behind you." Eyes on his prize, he added off-handedly, "See you at home, Lil."

It was so *good,* seeing him this happy! After Rose died, he'd sacrificed his whole life for his daughters;

if this woman could make him happy, Lily was all for it.

It seemed odd that romance was blooming all around her—Georgia had Robert, newlyweds Cammi and Reid had only recently returned from their honeymoon, even her father had found his match with the widow who lived next door. She didn't begrudge any of them their joy. Quite the opposite! It was just…why couldn't *she* have a slice of that kind of happiness?

She suddenly remembered what he'd said earlier, about Robert's freedom. *Because, you big idiot, you went and fell in love with this big galoot, and he thinks of marriage as a prison!*

"Ready?" Max said, offering her his arm.

Timidly, she took it, and walked beside him.

Beside him.

If she had her way, it's where she'd spend the rest of her days.

"Thank you, God!" Nate said, climbing into the back seat.

God.

Max was no longer a "follower," Lily recalled. What would it take to bring him back to the Lord? Prayer and faith had been responsible for Nate's now-healthy condition, and it was the reason Georgia's surgery had been such a success, too. Lily believed that with all her heart, so why couldn't Max see it!

During the drive to River Valley Ranch, Max pointed out landmarks to his son. Funny, touching, when-I-was-a-kid stories that made Lily smile. But her mind wasn't really on the old movie theater or the corner drugstore. It was on the future—one that she still couldn't imagine without Max in it.

Maybe finding someone who shared that rose-covered-cottage dream *and* her love of the Lord wouldn't be so hard, if only she'd let Max go. Maybe she ought to take Cammi's advice and move ahead without him.

Without him?

The very idea stung like a slap. Still, she couldn't—*wouldn't*—share her life with a man so stubbornly and deliberately separated from the Almighty.

"You're awfully quiet," Max said, reaching over the console to pat her hand. "You feelin' okay?"

"'Course I am." She'd answered too fast. Even she could hear the tension in her voice. "Why wouldn't I be?"

"Well, it's been a pretty hectic couple of weeks."

True. There'd been Cammi's wedding, Georgia's surgery and therapy, Nate's brush with death...and the new critters she'd added to her collection. She realized suddenly that this was a perfect time to express her faith. "Nothing I can't handle. It's all at the foot of the Cross."

One brow rose high on his forehead, one side of his mouth turned down slightly. His nonverbal message was clear: "Believe what you want. I don't fall for that nonsense anymore."

"My teacher at Sunday school in Chicago said that," Nate announced from the back seat. "She said if you give your troubles to God, He will help you through them."

Lily smiled over her shoulder. "She's absolutely right, Nate."

His adorable face crinkled with uncertainty. "Maybe. But I dunno."

Sensing he had more to say, she turned to see him better.

"I've been asking God for a mom for*ever,*" he said, hands extended in helpless supplication. "And when you found that dog? I talked to Him about that, too." Frowning, Nate slapped his hands on blue-jeaned thighs. "No mom, no dog. 'Nuff said."

"God doesn't always answer with a yes, Nate, but He always answers. *Always.*"

He thought about that for a minute. "So His answer is no?"

He looked so sad and disappointed. Lily didn't know what to say. *Help me, Lord. Speak through me so this little boy will grow in faith!* "I don't think He's saying yes or no. I think maybe He's saying 'wait.' When the time's right, if it's His will—"

"His will? What's that?"

What had she gotten herself in to? *Lord, don't fail me now!* she prayed. "Well, 'will' is…it's like a plan. Long before you were born, God knew you, knew what was best for you, too. And for as long as you live, He'll do everything in His power to see that you have what you need."

"What I need is a mom." And he added under his breath, "A dog would be nice, too."

Oh, if only *she* could fill the role of mom! He was adorable, big-hearted, and smarter than any four-year-old she'd ever met. And he was part of *Max.* No wonder she'd gone nuts over him!

She chanced a peek at Max, who stared stonily through the windshield. It dawned on her that Nate's remark had hurt his feelings, because he was trying his best to fill both roles. "Your dad does okay in the parent department, don't you think?"

Nate shrugged. "Yeah, I guess."

Max chuckled. "Careful, you two. My head gets any bigger from this onslaught of praise, I'll have to buy a convertible."

Lily faced front, discouraged with herself. Why hadn't she been able to tell Nate what he needed to hear? Perhaps because she wasn't cut out to be a mother, after all. Because if, as Cammi was always saying, she was a born nurturer, wouldn't the words have been there, on the tip of her tongue?

"So what kind of animals do you have in the barn?" Nate asked.

She said a quick prayer of thanks for the change of subject. "One hawk with a broken wing, an owl that's blind in one eye, a billy goat and a squirrel and a couple of monkeys…" She put a finger to her chin and squinted. "Hmm, seems I'm forgetting something."

"What about the dog?"

She couldn't help but notice how carefully he'd chosen his words. For an instant, she felt angry with Max for being so stubborn about a dog for his boy. But then, he'd been a dad for four years. Nate was living proof that he'd done a fine job, especially considering he'd done it alone. So who was she to question his parenting tactics!

No, clearly it had been her misconception—this idea that 'good mommy genes' flowed in her veins. Faced with cogent evidence that she didn't possess natural-born skills, after all, Lily was torn. On the one hand, this new revelation freed her to move in a different direction with her life; on the other, it required her to give up her dream. Not an easy undertaking, because, frankly, she'd grown pretty comfortable with it.

"That dog you found in the lake, I mean."

She forced a giggle. "Of course! How could I forget Missy?"

"Why'd you name her that?"

"Because we don't know how she got here, or where her owners are. She's a mystery. So I started calling her Miss Terry, Missy for short."

As his mother had when Lily explained the reasons behind the name choice, Max groaned. "I get it. 'Mys-tery.'" He shook his head. "That's reachin', Lil,' he teased. "*Really* reachin'."

He pulled into the long, ribboning lane that connected the highway to the house. "Place looks just as I remember it," Max said, parking in the circular drive.

"Wow," Nate said. "It's as big as the castle at Disney World!" He popped out of the car, sneakered feet thudding across the bridge's wide planks. "Look, Dad. A river!" he said, pointing.

"And Lily's dad put it there, with his own two hands," Max said. "Amazing, isn't it?"

Nate's voice was filled with amazement. "Yeah. I'll say."

Lily led the way to the barn, with Nate skipping on ahead and Max walking on her left. "Dad has never done anything halfway."

Max nodded. "My pop was the same way. He never built a river, mind you," he teased, "but he always said, 'Do your best or don't bother.' Didn't matter if I was cleaning my room or doing homework or mowing the lawn. 'It's a test of a man's character,' he'd tell me, 'to see what kind of work he'll put out when he thinks nobody's watching.'" Using his chin as a pointer, he nodded at Nate. "I'm trying to do for him what my dad did for me."

"You're doing a terrific job. Nate's a great kid, and he didn't get that way with smoke and mirrors."

"I'm trying," he said again. "But they're big shoes to fill," he said. "Real big."

"Your dad was a wonderful man," Lily agreed. She remembered Max's father from Youth Group at church. He'd volunteered one evening a week to run the program that allowed parish teens to gather for basketball or board games, movies in town, or just sit around, talking. He'd organized fund-raisers, picnics, collections for the needy, and taught "his kids" the importance of sharing not only their time, but themselves.

"My biggest regret," he said, "is that Nate will never meet him."

"And I'll bet he regrets not getting to know Nate. Hard not to love that kid."

Max stepped in front of her, blocking her path. She

didn't know what to make of the intense eye contact, didn't know how to read the silent message he sent on the invisible cable connecting their gazes.

"Dad! Lily!" Nate called. "I can hear 'em in there!"

The boy stood, ear pressed to the barn door, waving them forward. It was enough to get Lily's feet moving. "We'll have to be very quiet," she whispered, opening the door, "and move very slowly once we get inside, so we don't startle anybody."

Nate nodded, dark eyes bright with anticipation. Max looked pretty excited himself, Lily thought, smiling. As the threesome walked among the cages and stalls, Lily introduced them to her "patients."

Missy loped up, long golden fur rippling with each happy stride. She stopped just feet away from Nate, rear end in the air and tail wagging as she lowered her shoulders, an invitation to play.

His grin made it clear that he was more than happy to oblige. "Hi, girl," he said, kneeling on the straw-covered floor.

The dog nuzzled the crook of his neck. "Hey, that tickles!" he said, laughing so hard he lost his balance and rolled onto his side. "And your nose is cold!" he added. On his knees again, he hugged her. "I like you, Missy. You're fun!"

Max leaned his forearm on a stall door and shook his head. "Gonna be hard, makin' a clean getaway from here after *that* introduction."

So he'd made the decision, had he, that Nate couldn't have the dog? It was a shame…for Nate. But good for her, because she'd become very attached to the retriever.

Lamont's pup, Obnoxious, joined them, his quiet, breathy barks starting up a whole new fit of giggles in Nate. "Do *all* your dogs have cold noses?"

"These are the only dogs we have," Lily said. "And yes, most dogs have cold, wet snouts."

"Snouts," Nate giggled. "That's funny, Lily." He jumped up, grabbed Max's hand and asked, "Dad, Dad! Are we having ham for Thanksgiving dinner like we did last year?"

"Where did *that* come from?" Max said.

"Well, Lily said snouts, and pigs have snouts, and— I dunno. I just thought of it." He went back to playing with the dogs.

Lily frowned slightly. "Ham, instead of the traditional turkey dinner and all the trimmings?"

Max blushed guiltily. "Never learned how to roast a turkey, but ham I can do."

"Dad calls it our Canned Holiday feast, 'cause everything comes out of a can. 'Cept the gravy. That comes in a jar." He hid his grin behind both hands. "'Member how you forgot to thaw out the pun-kin pie last year?" A merry giggle punctuated the question. "And we had to slice it with the 'lectric knife? And how it crunched when we ate it? That was really funny, huh, Dad."

Max's blush deepened. "Yeah. A real memory-maker, all right." He lifted both shoulders and extended his hands, palm up. "I never claimed to be a French chef."

"Well, sounds to me like you did just fine, cooking

for two.'' Lily hoped, even as she said it, that Max would correct her, that he'd disagree and point out how many others had joined them at their holiday table. When he remained silent, she realized they'd spent the day alone.

Had they eaten *all* their holiday dinners that way?

The picture of the pair of them, huddled over a Formica table at Georgia's Diner, eating TV dinners or canned ham, upset her more than she could bear. And Georgia wasn't well enough yet to stand all day, basting the turkey, mixing up the stuffing, whipping potatoes….

''We always have a huge feast on Thanksgiving,'' Lily said, opening a can of dog food. ''You and Nate are more than welcome. Georgia and Robert, too, of course.'' She plopped the meat into a bowl near the one-eyed owl.

Nate looked up at her as if he believed she'd hung the moon. ''You mean a *real* turkey, with gravy and stuffing…and *everything?*''

Lily laughed. ''Yep. And a whole table full of desserts, too.'' To Max she said, ''Nadine always joins us, and she's bringing one of her sons and his family this year. It'll be great. A big old-fashioned fiesta!''

The boy wiggled his pointer finger, summoning his dad closer. ''Can we go, Dad?''

Max looked hesitant. ''You're sure it'll be all right with your dad?''

''Absolutely. 'The more, the merrier,' he always says.'' She spooned dog food into another container in the hawk's cage. ''Eat up, now,'' she crooned to it. "You have a long way to go before your wing is healed well enough for you to fly home."

The bird cocked its head, watching Lily first with one gleaming eye, then the other. As she scrubbed her hands, Lily said, "Maybe after dinner on Thursday, all you fellas can have yourselves a rousing game of football."

Father and son followed her around the barn, looking over her shoulder as she changed bandages, fed and watered every creature, and gave each one a moment of affection and one-on-one attention. Nate stared, open-mouthed, as she petted the one-eyed owl. "Aren't you scared he'll bite you? He has a very sharp beak."

"No," Lily said, stroking the feathered hunter's head, "because I've gotten to know him very well." To the owl, she said, "You would *never* bite me, would you?" In response, it merely blinked its golden eye.

Lily washed up again, and as she dried her hands she said, "How 'bout some hot chocolate, Nate? I make mine from scratch."

"Scratch? What's that?"

"It means 'not from a mix,'" Max offered.

"Is it better than the stuff in the little envelopes?"

"Way better." He chuckled. "What a great way to top off a cold Sunday evening."

Missy pranced alongside her as she led them down the flagstone path connecting the barn to the back porch, wondering as they went what they'd find to talk about while she prepared the cocoa, while they sipped it.

"I like Lily, Dad...."

Lily knew she wasn't supposed to have heard that; the boy had done his four-year-old best to whisper.

"...and not just 'cause she's pretty, either."

It was all she could do to keep from turning around to see how Max had reacted to *that*.

"Ditto," he said.

"Ditto? What's 'ditto,' Dad?"

"It means 'I feel the same way.'"

He hadn't lowered his voice, hadn't even attempted to keep her from hearing him, Lily noticed.

For the moment, she forgot the promise she'd made to herself. Dismissed the possibility that Max was just being "nice." Why not enjoy the possibility that he had feelings for her that went beyond the boundaries of friendship—just for the moment, of course.

"Is Missy allowed in the house?"

"Sure," Lily said over her shoulder.

"My friend in Chicago had a dog but it wasn't allowed inside. Which was weird, 'cause he had a big ol' green lizard with pointy things on his back, and his mom let him keep *that* in his bedroom!"

What would they talk about?

Something told her that with Nate around, topics of conversation wouldn't be a problem.

Max's quiet, masculine laughter floated on the chilly November breeze as Lily bit her lower lip to keep from saying *Thank you, Lord!* out loud.

Chapter Seven

The kitchen was warm with the scents and sounds of festive Thanksgiving preparation. On the stove, lids danced atop steaming pots, while on the counter, loaves of home-baked bread, rolls and biscuits, blanketed with blue-striped towels, sat in orderly rows. The timer *ding*ed, and Lily put down the potato peeler to grab an oven mitt.

Max had intended to join her here, and offer to help if he could. But in the minute or so since he'd rounded the corner, he'd stood, mesmerized. It surprised him to see Lily alone in the room, handling each womanly chore with deft precision; he'd expected to find all three of the London girls in there with her, laughing and talking as they put the finishing touches on the Thanksgiving banquet. Surprised, but relieved, because this way, he could watch her unnoticed.

She'd piled her long, thick hair atop her head with a green plastic band that matched her shirt. Wisps of hair that had escaped the upsweep curled in the hollow at the back of her neck; a few more formed bouncy ringlets beside her ears. He'd give anything to press a gentle kiss to those lovely lobes.

After painting the turkey with a thick coat of melted butter, she covered it with a tent made of aluminum foil and closed the oven door. The bracelet he'd given her caught a beam of light, forcing his attention to her slender wrist. Max wouldn't mind placing a soft kiss there, either.

Suddenly, she began humming a tune he hadn't heard since boyhood. Smiling, he pocketed his hands and leaned on the door frame. He'd forgotten what a beautiful voice she had. Crossing one booted ankle in front of the other, he listened, captivated by her voice, her movements. She was a vision, a dream come to life.

"'Over the river and through the woods,'" she sang. Then, without looking up, she said, "You remember the words, Max, feel free to sing along."

Chuckling, he shook his head. "How long have you known I was here?"

When she met his eyes, his heart thumped and his stomach lurched. She was ravishing, what with her heat-pinked cheeks and big green eyes. And that smile… She could charm the leaves from the trees with that smile, Max thought.

"Not long," she said.

Something told him she'd seen him the instant he'd appeared in the doorway, and she'd only said "not long" to spare him any embarrassment. Even as a kid, Lily had gone out of her way to make others feel good, even if it meant taking it on the chin herself. And he'd always loved her for that.

Loved? No, Max admitted. Nothing past tense about it.

He took a few steps closer. "Anything I can do to help?"

She cocked her head, gave it a moment's thought. "As a matter of fact, there is."

"Your wish is my command," he said. He bowed, more to keep her from reading his emotions than to emulate a gentleman. Because there was no getting around it: Max didn't think he could deny her anything, ever. *Just part of the problem,* he admitted. Years ago, love for Lily had made him feel guilty, because even at eighteen, he'd known how inappropriate his feelings for her were because of their age difference. He'd been too young, too immature back then to understand what motivated his reaction to her. But he understood it now. Her father had been right when he'd said her heart was as big as her head. Even as a callow youth, Max had sensed that she was good—that she'd be good for *him.*

"You can go into the dining room, see how Cammi and Violet and Ivy are doing. They swore they could fit all twenty-six of us at the table, and I'm dying to find out how they did it...if they did it!"

Much as he wanted to do what she'd asked, Max couldn't leave the kitchen. It felt good in here, cozy and comfortable. "Why don't we just wait 'til it's time to put stuff on the table. Let it be a surprise."

"I've never been too keen on surprises." She held

up the paring knife, used it as a pointer and grinned. "You can peel potatoes, instead, if you'd rather."

Laughing, Max held up his hands and ducked out the door, saying, "I'll be back in a second."

"Thank you!" he heard her say as he stepped into the dining room.

Immediately, he could see that her sisters had been busy. The already-long dining room table where he'd shared many a Sunday dinner as a boy had been lengthened even more by the addition of two card tables at each end. Their thin brown-painted legs looked weak and flimsy by comparison to the sturdy light oak that supported the main table. China, crystal and silver glinted in the light of the ornate chandelier overhead. Mismatched chairs, mixed among those that matched the table, lent a casual warmth to the elegance.

Lily was whipping potatoes when he returned to the kitchen. "Couldn't find them," he reported, stepping up beside her. "But the job's done and it looks great. Only thing missing is food."

She spooned a dollop of sour cream into the mashed spuds. "Mmm, perfect," she said over the *whir* of the electric mixer. "Would you do me one more favor—ask the girls to come help me put the food on the buffet?"

"You bet."

"Thanks, Max."

He tucked a tendril of hair behind her ear, allowed his crooked finger to graze her lightly freckled cheek. Max leaned close and kissed it, lingering for an instant because she smelled like flowers and line-dried sheets and sweet butter.

Lily stiffened slightly at first, and just when he thought she'd tell him to back off, she faced him and, closing her eyes, invited him to kiss her again—for real this time.

It was an offer he couldn't refuse.

The moment pulsed and crackled, like the energy that surged through the cord, powering the mixer. She must have felt it, too, for she sighed and leaned closer, lifting the appliance from the deep pot as she did.

Egg-size blobs of mashed potatoes spun loose from the beaters and landed *splat,* on Max's shoulder, on her cheek, on his forehead, on the back of her hand. Lips still pressed to his, she began to giggle. "Maybe we should share some of this with the rest of them."

"No way," he said, a forefinger to her full lower lip. "This is mine. All mine."

Her smile vanished like smoke as she blinked up at him. What was going on in that pretty head of hers? he wondered. One thing was certain, the magic of the moment had disappeared. "Well, guess I'll round up the relatives and herd them into the dining room."

One delicate brow rose slightly as the hint of a grin lifted the corners of her lovely lips. "I'll turn you loose, then," she said, though one hand still held the mixer, the other the pot handle.

She had it all—a big heart, looks, brains, too many talents to list, and a sense of humor, too. "If I have the sense God gave a goose, I wouldn't let you get away this time."

He saw her swallow, heard her quick intake of air

as she looked left, right…anywhere but into his eyes. "Well," she started, "I, um…"

Difficult as it was to let her go, Max pocketed his hands and headed for the door. "How long 'til soup's on?" he said from the hall.

She cleared her throat. Touched fingertips to her lips. "Five minutes." She looked away, then met his eyes to add, "Ten at most."

Nodding, he walked away smiling to himself. His kiss had rattled her. Because she hadn't expected it? Because she had enjoyed it every bit as much as he had? A frown replaced the smile at his last thought: Because she'd finally figured out he wasn't right for her?

His heart had pounded during that kiss, but not half as hard as it hammered at *that* possibility. He walked into the family room, saw his son frolicking with Missy as the adults discussed the weather, politics, who'd win today's football game.

"London girls," he said, standing at attention and saluting, "report for kitchen duty."

When the laughter ended, Cammi, Violet and Ivy hurried to the kitchen. "You're such a nut!" Cammi said as she passed him.

"Y'gotta love a guy with a sense of humor," Ivy chimed in.

His practiced smile hid the truth. He'd spent the past six years pretending to look happy. Obviously, since no one ever gave a hint they suspected his joviality was an act, he'd gotten pretty good at it.

What would it take, he asked himself as the ladies filed by, to make him happy…*truly* happy?

Lily stuck her head out the kitchen door and smiled, waving her sisters into the room. "I thought you'd abandoned ship!" she teased. "Everything's ready—just needs to be put on the buffet."

"You're terrific, Lil," Ivy said.

"But really, you should have let us help more," Vi agreed. "I don't know why you insisted on doing it all yourself."

"I know why," Cammi singsonged. "To show a certain…"

Her voice trailed off as she ducked into the kitchen, preventing Max from hearing the end of Cammi's sentence. But it didn't take a genius to figure out who Lily was trying to impress. So, had he misread her reaction when he'd cracked the "I wouldn't let you get away" remark?

He hoped so. Because he knew exactly what would make him happy, now and until he breathed his last.

Being with Lily, that's what.

"Dinner was great, Lily," Georgia said. "If I'd known you could cook like that, Andy's job would have been in jeopardy!"

Lily blushed and rolled her eyes. "Please. You never would have agreed to let me put paper doilies under the pies and cakes…too fancy for your truck driver clientele."

Laughing, Georgia said, "You make a good point." She turned to Robert and said, "Now?"

Grinning like a schoolboy, the doctor got to his feet, clinked the handle of his butter knife on his water goblet. "Excuse me. Ahem. May I have your attention, please?"

One by one, they stopped talking to look his way.

"I have an announcement to make. Or rather," he said, one hand on Georgia's shoulder, "*we* have an announcement."

Max leaned toward Lily. "Here it comes," he whispered, "the moment we've all been waiting for."

"Robert asked me to marry him," his mother said, fanning her face with her napkin, "and I said yes."

The instant of silence was broken when Lily applauded. "Congratulations, you two!" she said, hurrying to their side of the table. She gave each of them a hug, a kiss on the cheek. "What wonderful, wonderful news!"

"I agree," Max said, joining them. "It's about time, *Dad*," he added, jacking Robert's arm up and down like a pump handle.

"Does that mean you're my grandpa?" Nate asked.

Robert said, "Yep, it sure does."

Lily and Max returned to their seats as Lamont stood. "Time for the traditional London family thank-you list." He looked from Robert to Max, from Georgia to Nadine's son and his family. "For those of you who've never joined us for Thanksgiving dinner, we have this ritual. Nobody gets dessert 'til they've shared one thing they're thankful for." He faced Lily. "Sweetie, why don't you show 'em how it's done."

She sat back, hands folded primly in her lap, and said, "I'm thankful that every one of you is part of my life." She faced Lamont. "Your turn, Dad."

When it was Cammi's turn, she grabbed Reid's

hand. "I'm grateful to have the husband of my dreams to wake up to every morning."

Nate said, "I'm thankful for having Lily's blood in me, 'cause maybe it'll make me into a good vettin-air-yun when I grow up."

So much for "save the best for last," Max thought, because now it was his turn. He'd never been much good at public speaking, and this came close enough. It made him nervous, made his voice waver, his hands shake and his ears hot—and an icy sensation snaked down his back. "Truth is, I have a lot to be thankful for," he said. But if he had to single out one thing, as everyone else had, what would it be?

I rediscovered Lily, he thought.

"How utterly romantic!" Ivy gushed.

"That's one of the sweetest things I've ever heard," Vi agreed.

Ivy and Vi had been confusing him since high school. Now, their identical faces lit up as if they were still teenagers! Until the twins spoke up, Max hadn't realized he'd said aloud what he'd been thinking. How was he going to dig himself out of *this* one!

His mouth was suddenly bone dry, his palms damp. He reached for his water glass and missed, spilling it across the tabletop and into Lily's lap. "Aw, man. I'm such a clod," he said, attempting to blot it with his napkin.

But she leaned forward at the same moment he had, and his chin connected with her eye.

Instantly, Lily's hand covered the spot. "Self-defense," he said, groaning inwardly. "Not that I blame you." He slid his chair closer to hers, put an arm around her. "I'm sorry, Lily. Man. I'm batting a thousand, aren't I. You okay? Lemme see."

"I have a hard head," she said, smiling good-naturedly. "I'm fine."

But she wasn't. A tiny trickle of blood had already started creeping toward her cheek. "You're not fine. You're bleeding!" He grabbed his napkin, dipped it into her glass and tried to daub the tiny cut. Nate chose that moment to get a closer look and bumped Max's elbow, causing him to poke Lily in the eye, instead.

"Good grief, Max," his mother said, "stop helping her before you *really* hurt her!"

"He didn't mean it, Georgia," Nadine said. "Men sometimes get clumsy around girls they're sweet on." She pointed at a bruise on her forearm. "Got his one when Lamont tried to help me out of the car the other day." She showed them a scratch on the opposite elbow. "And this is from when he boosted me into the saddle when we went riding the other day."

A smattering of laughter punctuated her story. "You know what they say—'love hurts,'" Lamont said, chuckling.

Their banter did little to ease Max's guilt. He sat back, shoulders sagging, as Lily excused herself.

"I'll just be a minute, guys. Help yourselves to dessert, why don't you!"

Max rose halfway, intending to pull out her chair. At the last second, he decided against it, for fear he'd trip her with one of its legs. Not until she was safely out of the room did he get up. The others were busy pointing to which dessert they'd like to cut into first; he hoped no one would notice he'd left the table.

He stepped outside, quietly closing the huge front door behind him, and took a deep breath. The sky mirrored his mood—cold and gray. He sat on the top step of the porch and leaned both elbows on his knees, staring across the vast expanse of lawn that made up the London front yard. Shaking his head, he ran a hand through his hair. "Klutz," he grumbled. "Bumbling idiot. Clumsy oaf."

"Don't be so hard on yourself."

Her sudden appearance on the porch startled him, and he lurched slightly. "How long have you been standing there?"

"Not long," she said, reminding them of their earlier conversation in the kitchen. She sat down beside him, held the hair back from her temple. "See? No big deal. It's just a teeny tiny little—"

He groaned, aloud this time. "Aw, man. You're gonna have a big ugly knot on your head by morning." Wincing, he added, "Sorry, Lil."

She nudged him with her shoulder. "Accidents happen, Max."

He looked into her face, saw that she'd meant every word. Max couldn't help but chuckle at the situation—he'd clocked her, not the other way around, yet Lily was comforting *him!* No doubt about it: Happiness could be his for the asking...if only he could figure out how to ask.

Max slid an arm around her, gave her a little sideways hug. "You're something else, you know that?"

He felt her shrug, heard her sigh.

"What?" he said.

But she only shook her head.

"Headache?"

"No."

He wasn't so sure. It would be just like her to hide any discomfort he'd caused her.

As if she'd read his mind, she looked at him just then. "Honest," she said, patting his thigh. "I'm fine."

She didn't take her hand back, he noticed, but let it lie there instead, warming not only the skin beneath it, but his entire being. Maybe he should just 'fess up. Tell her how he felt.

Then again, maybe he shouldn't; knowing Lily, she'd echo his words, if only to spare his feelings. Because, really, what did a gorgeous li'l gal like her want with a guy like him? A union between them, well, it was all in his favor. He'd get a pretty, big-hearted wife, Nate would get a loving mom—and what would Lily get? He glanced at her, saw that the spot where his chin had connected with her temple was already bruising. A lot of hard work, he thought, answering his own question—and contusions and abrasions.

She shivered.

"Let's go inside," he said, standing. And looking at the darkening sky, Max quoted Shakespeare: "'Something wicked this way comes...'" He held out his hand to help her up, and she willingly put hers into it. "You're a brave, trusting soul, aren't you," he teased.

"Either that," she shot back, "or a glutton for punishment."

He cringed. "Oooh. Cheap shot. But I guess I had it coming. That, and then some."

She stood in his path and, hands on her hips, said, "You have plenty coming, Max Sheridan, but it's all good stuff, 'cause you're a good man."

My, but she was gorgeous standing there, green eyes flashing, long dark hair billowing in the breeze.

"You're kind and hardworking and decent, right down to the very core of you!" She emphasized the point by jabbing a finger into his chest.

"You think so, huh?"

She tidied the collar of his shirt, in a gesture he could only call "wifely."

"No. I don't think so, I *know* so."

"Well," he said hoarsely, taking her in his arms, "if I'm so good and decent, why is it that every time I look at you, I want to kiss the daylights out of you?"

He heard her tiny gasp, saw her big eyes widen further as he slid his arms around her. She hadn't stiffened this time, he noticed, the way she had in the kitchen while she mashed potatoes, and his wild emotions flew about. Could it mean she felt the same way he did—that happiness, genuine happiness, could be found right here in one another's arms? Was that too much to ask for? If he was a praying man, he'd ask the Almighty to intervene, right now, on his behalf.

Instead, he buried his face in her hair and held her tight, so tightly that not even the frosty wind could have squeaked between them. *Ah, Lily,* he thought, eyes closed as he inhaled the sweetly feminine scents clinging to her soft tresses, *if only I could—*

She bracketed his face with her hands and forced him to meet her eyes. "They're eating up all the dessert without us, you know."

He smiled. What did he care? In his opinion, the sweetest thing ever made was standing right here in his arms. "Probably."

Hands on his shoulders now, she said, "We'll be lucky if there are even crumbs left for us."

"Maybe…"

"Funny, I'm not cold anymore."

"Me, neither." But then, he hadn't been cold to start with.

"Think they've even noticed we're gone?"

"No doubt in my mind. The room temperature likely dropped twenty degrees when you left, 'cause you're warm as the sun."

She batted her lashes and gave his chest a playful smack. "Cut it out. You're gonna make me blush."

Max studied her face for a quiet moment. He memorized every detail, from the perfectly arched feminine brows to the gently sloping freckled nose to the generous pink lips. Those wonderful, velvety soft lips…

"You planning to kiss me again, or just stand there, staring at my mouth?"

He almost laughed because, once again, she'd read his mind. There wasn't another woman like her, not in all the world.

"All right, then," she said, tucking in one corner

of that tantalizing mouth, "I guess I'll have to take the bull by the horns."

She stood on tiptoe and, one hand on either side of his face again, kissed him. Kissed him like she meant it, right down to her toes. It seemed like a fog had descended on him, blotting out rational thought, blocking common sense. He struggled to work his way out of it, so he could tell her *with words* that she was the answer to his every prayer.

Prayer? *That* brought him back to the Land of the Thinking, because Max hadn't prayed in years. He ended the dizzying contact, held her at arm's length. She looked so starry-eyed that he had to fight the impulse to kiss her again. "You just saved me a ton of empty calories," he said, his voice gravelly and gruff, even to his own ears. So he cleared his throat and smiled. "My waistline thanks you."

She only stood there, blinking, a faint smile shining in her eyes.

"Guess we'd better get back inside, before your father sends Obnoxious out here to tear my throat out."

Lily laughed. "Obnoxious is quite literally all bark and no bite. You're safe as a babe in his mother's arms with that pup."

Max stood beside her, draped an arm over her shoulders. "Looks like rain."

"Mmm…"

"Hope it won't be the thunder and lightning kind. Nate is terrified of storms."

She was quiet for a minute, and then she said,

"Well, I have a feeling you handle that just as well as you handle everything else."

He opened the door, held it for her. *The girl sure is good for what ails a man,* Max thought as she stepped into the foyer. In the weeks he'd been back in Amarillo, she'd awakened emotions in him he'd forgotten existed. It amazed him that some good-lookin' dude hadn't come along, snapped her up, made her his bride.

He closed the door harder than he'd intended, bristling at the thought of Lily married to another man, having his kids, sharing his life.

"What's wrong?"

Max looked at her. "Wrong? Nothing. Why?"

"Well, you look so—" she frowned, searching for the right word "—a cross between horrified and furious."

That pretty well described it, all right. "Ate too much, that's all."

"So you really don't want dessert? Georgia told me your favorite sweet treat is Dutch apple pie."

Lily looked downright disappointed, which meant she'd baked one, just for him. Max's heart melted at the realization that she'd sought out yet another way to show him she cared. It wasn't her fault, was it, that all his life he'd pretended to love the stuff rather than hurt his mother's feelings? "Well," he said, holding his thumb and forefinger an inch apart, "maybe just a small slice." Max patted his stomach. "Any more and I'm liable to explode."

Her exquisite face brightened and her voice went back to its usual melodic tones. "Sounds like everyone has retreated to the family room. Go on in and make yourself comfy while I get it for you.'' She headed for the corner of dining room, where no fewer than a dozen delectable treats lined the sideboard. ''Go on,'' she said, motioning him onward. ''I'll be right in.''

Just like that, she was out of sight. Max thought he knew how Noah must have felt when God turned off the sun and started the clouds to raining on the sinful earth, because she'd taken the warmth and brightness with her.

You must be crazy, Max told himself, *not snapping her up yourself, years ago.* Wasn't like he hadn't thought about it, dozens of times. All he needed to do was head back to Texas, make sure he ran into her, start up where they'd left off. So many times, he'd almost asked his mother how Lily was doing— if she'd fallen in love, married, started a family. Hearing that news would have cut like a saber, so he hadn't asked. Nothing could have surprised him more than learning none of those things had happened. Any man would consider himself blessed to have her as his wife!

Blessed? What was with him today, he wondered, remembering that minutes ago, he'd thought about prayer.

Not so surprising, really, that he'd have heavenly things on his mind. In his opinion, Lily was his own personal messenger from God.

Chapter Eight

Max took the only seat left in the family room, beside Lamont. The man was impressive in so many ways that he could be downright intimidating, and Max had never been sure—not as a boy and certainly not now—whether Lamont meant folks to read him that way.

Behind his back, people sometimes called Lamont "John Wayne," not for his rolling gait, but for his tough, no-nonsense way of communicating. That style had commanded the respect and admiration of bankers and cowboys alike—and had helped make Lamont London one of the wealthiest men in the Texas Panhandle.

Years ago, Max had walked into the barbershop just as Lamont was leaving. "Now, there's a man y'don't want to cross," said one man. "They don't call him The Griz for nothin'," said another. Months later, Max saw with his own eyes what they'd been talking about when Lamont lit into a cashier for short-changing him and denying it.

Max wondered which of Lamont's daughters had inherited his fiery temper. Definitely not Lily, and from what he could see, not Cammi, either. Left to decide between the twins, Max would choose Violet over Ivy. He looked at her now, perched on the arm of the sofa nearest her date, arms crossed over her chest, chin up and left eyebrow raised as she surveyed the goings-on in the room, while Cammi and Ivy giggled and chattered, like a couple of cartoon chipmunks.

Better watch it, bud, he warned himself. *These people could be your in-laws some day.*

Max almost laughed out loud at the thought. He'd shared, what, half a dozen kisses with Lamont's youngest girl? Even if Lily was, in his opinion, perfect, enchanting, a *gift,* they were a long way from marriage.

Right?

He did some surveying of his own in the London family room.

Max supposed Robert had felt the same unease before asking Georgia to marry him. Reid likely had experienced some angst before proposing to Cammi. Even Lamont appeared ready to take the plunge…but hadn't.

He may not yet have popped the question, but could that be far off? Because *something* major had changed about Lamont in the years Max had been away, and he suspected Nadine Greene had everything to do with it. Lamont laughed at Nadine's jokes, looked long into her eyes, clung to her every word—and she mirrored the loving, affectionate behavior. A far cry from the growly, grumpy man who'd earned the nickname "The Griz"!

If love could tame a man like Lamont, Max knew he didn't stand a chance.

But…did he *want* a chance?

He'd been thinking wacky, crazy thoughts since coming back to Amarillo, things like how great life would be with Lily, and what a terrific wife and mother she'd be.

Then again, when Lily had pointed out that Georgia and Robert would be happy together, he'd raised her hackles with his "grass is greener" remark.

So which was it? Did he want his freedom or didn't he?

It was a question he'd better think about, long and hard, and soon.

She came into the room carrying a pie plate in one hand, a cup of coffee in the other. "It's decaf," she said, putting them on the end table beside him. She pulled a napkin-wrapped fork out of her pocket, handed it to him.

"Looks terrific," he said. And it did, too—golden-brown crust, perfectly sliced cinnamony apple wedges. "Thanks."

She patted his shoulder. "I'll be in the kitchen if you need anything." And with that, she hurried off.

Her sisters soon joined her, followed by Nadine and her daughter-in-law and Max's cane-toting mother. A minute passed before Nadine's son said, "Amazing how much noise women can make, isn't it?"

Reid laughed. "Much as I hate to admit it, Adam, you make a good point."

"Why, I didn't even notice the racket, 'til the racket-eers were gone," Robert joked.

Nate came over, sat on Max's knee and pointed tentatively at the pie. "You gonna eat that?"

"No," he said, sliding the plate toward him. "Help yourself."

"Thanks, Dad!" On his knees at the coffee table, Nate gobbled a few bites and smacked his lips. "Mmm. Delicious. Lily's a good cook, too."

Meaning, Max thought, in addition to her other qualities and talents. And there were plenty, all right. He glanced around the room again, at the faces of the contented, cheerful men whose lives had been made better because they'd chosen the right women. Must be nice, he thought, starting every day knowing there was someone beside them—a partner to share life's ups and downs, its joy and sadness.

When these guys left for work every morning, each took with him the knowledge that his toil had a purpose, that the responsibility of caring for his loved ones wasn't a burden, but a pleasure. And when he came home again at night, someone would be waiting, and she'd welcome him home with a warm hug and a warmer kiss.

But he wouldn't turn on the TV because he'd much rather sit in the kitchen pretending to read the newspaper, watching as she puttered, checked the doneness of things, hummed to herself, all while looking pretty in the gold *X*s and *O*s bracelet he'd bought her. And somewhere along the way she'd press her soft hands to his face and smile sweetly, and after another delicious kiss, tell him she'd baked his favorite pie for dessert. And even though it wasn't *really* his favorite pie, he'd eat it, because—

Whoa. How had *he* gotten involved in the scene?

Max checked to make sure he hadn't drooled. Wouldn't have surprised him at all to find that he had! *You're losin' it, pal.* He'd better get a grip soon.

He wondered exactly what would happen if he *didn't* get a grip. Would he get down on one knee, take Lily's hand in his, slide a diamond on her finger? Or would he simply tell her, in plain English, that he thought they'd make a perfect pair? Nodding to himself, Max thought, Yeah, that was definitely more his style.

He sat back and stared at the TV screen, where two NFL teams were going at it on the field. At the moment, he couldn't remember who wore green and yellow and who wore purple, but he sure could identify with the guy who'd fumbled the ball!

Max couldn't remember feeling more confused. Couldn't think of a time when he'd felt this addle-brained. What was going on?

Who was he kidding? He knew what was going on. If love could do *this* to a man, he didn't know if he wanted any part of it.

Then again, that whole little kitchen scene he'd just dreamed up had been awfully nice....

"What's your problem?" Robert asked him. "You look kinda green around the gills."

Max tried to smile. "Ate too much, I guess."

Robert nodded at the pie plate. "Good thing Nate likes your mama's pie." He wrinkled his nose. "I love her more than life itself, but…"

Max shuddered. "I've been chokin' the stuff down since I was a boy. Maybe one of these days I'll screw up the courage to tell her I'd rather eat raw muskrat."

The men laughed, each sharing a similar story.

"Why do we do it?" Adam asked. "They're sure quick enough to find fault."

"Not Georgia," Robert said.

"Never heard a word of complaint from Cammi," Reid agreed.

Lamont shrugged. "Nadine's pretty good at takin' it on the chin. If she has a beef, she hasn't shared it with me."

They looked at Max. "Well?" Robert said.

He cleared his throat. "Well, what?"

Groaning and laughing, the men shot "cut it out" and "oh brother" his way. "You know what we're talkin' about," Robert said. He extended his hands, palm up, wiggled his fingertips. "Give."

Give what? Some concocted story that made him part of the group? He *wasn't* part of the group! He and Lily were friends.

Max remembered those kisses they'd shared on the front porch earlier. Okay, so they were *good* friends. That didn't mean they were a couple, that they'd spent enough time together, alone, to discover one another's faults, or lack of them.

"Yeah," Adam said, "give."

"I—I, uh, well…"

He felt like the stuff between the proverbial rock and the hard place: There sat Lily's father, looking his grizzly best. Her brother-in-law Reid mirrored the expression. Even his future stepfather sat on the edge of his seat. Max didn't know whether to be amused or angry, because why did any of them care one way or the other!

"Sorry," he said, shoulders up and hands out, "we just don't have that kind of relationship." For Lamont's benefit, he quickly added "Yet," though for the life of him he couldn't say why.

Before the night was over, he might just find himself in the middle of a "what are your intentions toward my daughter" conversation. And to be honest, Max didn't think he was ready for that. Didn't know if he'd ever be ready for that. If he was smart, he'd start looking for reasons Lily *wouldn't* be good for his life, instead of compiling a long, unwieldy list of reasons she would. But then, if he was smart, would he be here, feeling uncomfortable because he had no story to tell?

Nate looked up at him, licking the caramel-colored goo that holds apple pie together from his lips. The boy smiled, saying with his expression that he thought his dad was awesome. He could see himself having a couple more kids, just like this one, who'd look up to him that way...

"That pie was great, Dad. Thanks." Nate got to his feet and picked up the plate and fork. "I'm gonna take this to the kitchen, so Lily won't have to come back for it."

Suddenly, the others began collecting china and silver and heading for the kitchen. He only hoped the boy wouldn't tell Lily *he* had eaten the pie she'd baked especially for Max, because it might hurt her feelings. He winced. He didn't want that.

Now everyone gathered in the kitchen.

Everyone but Max, that is.

He sat, slumped in the chair that matched Lamont's, staring at a commercial geared more to humor than to selling a product. But he wasn't getting the intended joke. His mind was such a muddle, he wasn't getting much of *anything*. Resting his head on the chair's back cushion, he slapped both hands over his face.

"Not feeling well?"

Lily…

Max opened his eyes, tried a smile on for size. It didn't fit, but he kept it on, anyway. "Hey. I didn't hear you come in." Did his cheeriness sound as phony to her as it did to him? Max hoped not.

"It's a talent," she said, perching on the arm of his chair.

He noticed suddenly that she held a dessert plate in one hand, a silver fork in the other. *Uh-oh,* he thought, it was just as he had feared: *Nate spilled the beans.*

"I understand Dutch apple isn't your favorite pie, after all."

Funny, she didn't sound hurt.

"Seems a shame to go without dessert." She leaned across him to put the plate on the end table. "I want you to know," Lily added, smiling *exactly* the way he'd pictured her in that daydream a little while ago, ''I think it's sweet, the way you've been eating something you don't like all these years, just to spare your mom's feelings.'' She leaned in again, pressed a kiss to his temple. ''Do me a favor?''

He glanced at the plate. Chocolate cake. Looked homemade, too. He'd only picked at his dinner, and Nate had eaten his pie… Max licked his lips and forced himself to meet her eyes. ''Favor? Sure. Anything.'' This time when he smiled, he meant it.

''Don't ever do that to me, okay?''

He frowned, shook his head. ''I'm not following you.''

''Don't ever pretend you like something, just to please me. I'd much rather *really* please you.''

She tilted her head when she said it, flirty-like. And her smile went from sweet to kind of mischievous. Max didn't quite know what to make of that.

Mmm…so therein lies the rub, he thought. *She* thought of them as a couple, too. *That's what you get, idiot, for kissing her like you meant it.*

But he *had* meant it, hadn't he?

''Promise?''

Promise what? Promise he meant it? Or promise not to say he liked pie if he didn't? By now, he honestly didn't know for sure, but Max nodded, feeling like one of those back-car-window doggies. ''Sure. I promise.''

Earlier, he'd assessed the changes in Lamont, thought that if love could change a man that much, maybe he ought to try it. *Maybe you ought to think again,* he decided. Because this whole ''love'' thing was turning him into a bumbling, babbling, half-wit.

''Do you like chocolate cake?''

His gaze darted to the thick wedge beside him. ''Well, yeah!'' He laughed and grabbed the plate. ''Who doesn't?'' His mouth began to water because now he could smell the delicious richness of it.

''You're not just saying that, to be nice....''

She tilted her head again, and suddenly he didn't know which sweet treat had started him salivating. ''I'll be honest,'' he started, using the fork as a pointer, ''I don't know if I want to jam this whole thing into my mouth at once, or kiss you.''

Lily tipped her head back a bit and laughed. She gave his shoulder a playful shove. ''The cake will get stale if you don't eat it soon, but there's plenty of time for—'' she wiggled her eyebrows ''—for the other.'' With that, she hopped off the chair arm and walked toward the door.

Max stuffed a forkful of cake into his mouth. ''Aw, man,'' he said around it. ''This is terrific.''

She stopped long enough to say, ''Glad you like it.''

''Homemade?''

''Yup. My mama's recipe.'' And she disappeared around the corner.

''Max,'' he said to himself, slicing off another bite of the cake, ''your boy's right...the girl can cook.''

And she genuinely enjoyed cooking for *him*. If he told her how he felt, Lily would reciprocate. Max knew that, as well as he knew his own name. As the fudgy frosting melted on his tongue, he realized he'd better get his head together. It wasn't fair to Lily to string her along. She deserved the best, *only* the best. No doubt she'd be good for him, for Nate.

But Max had been on his own a long time, doing things his way, in his own good time. Could he change? Could he open up and welcome her into his world?

Did he *want* to?

He ate another chunk of cake. Yeah, he did.

Those kisses on the porch echoed in his memory again. She was like no woman he'd ever met. Honest and straightforward, hardworking, with—how had Lamont put it again?—a heart as big as her head.

With a heart like that, she could put up with any nonsense he and Nate might dish out. But what about *her?* What could he and Nate offer Lily?

That's what he needed to ask. It was only fair, after all, to force her to peek over the legendary "fence," see that the grass might not be as green as it seemed, especially considering she'd been looking over there since junior high.

Did he love Lily?

Yeah, big time.

Was he *in love* with her?

Definitely. No doubt about it.

Enough to spend the rest of his life with her?

The question echoed in his mind, a moment, another...

Enough to spend the rest of my life with her?

That welcome-home kitchen scene he'd conjured earlier flashed in his head—beautiful, loving Lily at the stove, singing a tune under her breath, telling him "I've made your favorite."

Suddenly, the fantasy grew. Two more kids in the kitchen with Nate, laughing, running in circles around a high chair, where a baby squealed with delight, banging a big wooden spoon on the tray. In this version, Lily's stomach was swollen with child...*his* child. She wanted to name this one after his dad, if it was a boy. It's only fair, she was saying, since he'd let her name the last one Rose, for her mom.

It didn't have to be an illusion. It could be every bit as real as the cake crumbs on the plate in his hands.

Did he want that?

Max stood. Like his son, he'd take the plate to the kitchen, to spare Lily having to come fetch it. He saw her the minute he stepped into the family-crowded, brightly lit room, bent at the waist to wipe cake crumbs from Nate's mouth. She took the boy's face in both hands and rubbed her nose against his, then kissed his forehead. And the kid responded by wrapping his arms around her waist.

Yeah, he wanted that. Wanted *her,* more than anything.

Lessons his dad had taught him rang in Max's head. A man can't take his happiness at the expense of others. Do what's right, even if it hurts. *Earn* what you want.

That last bit of advice reverberated. Max nodded, realizing *that* had been the missing puzzle piece. Lily had loved him for what seemed like forever, but what had he done to earn it?

Nothing.

All the more reason to love her, because she'd

handed over her heart, and would hand over her life if he asked her to, without so much as a hint of "what's in it for me?"

Well, there ought to be something in it for her. *Had* to be something for her.

He'd make a point of spending more time with her, let her get to know the *real* Max Sheridan—not the one she'd been looking at all these years over that legendary "fence."

Scary concept, he thought, because what if Lily discovered he wasn't anything like the Max she'd fantasized about since girlhood?

It was a risk he had to take, for her sake.

And if things worked out as he hoped they would, it was how he'd earn her love.

Chapter Nine

Lily loved spending time with Max and Nate. They'd been together a lot lately. Twice, sometimes three times a week, they'd drop by to watch her feed the animals. Nate warmed to the monkeys, and they to him, so she allowed him to feed them fruit and vegetables. She found herself drawn to Georgia's Diner, too, and not for the food!

Now, she sat at the counter while Max whistled off-key, flipping burgers as Andy watched over him like a mother hen. Did he like helping out in the diner as his mom recuperated? Or would he rather be back in Chicago, rubbing elbows with rich, powerful clients at the accounting firm?

It wasn't the first time the questions had come to mind, but things always seemed to prevent her asking them. Things like…did the Windy City remind him of his marriage to Melissa, her suicide?

Lily might have asked him now, if the phone hadn't rung.

His peaceful expression turned stony and stern when he recognized the caller's voice. His tense tone told her the conversation wasn't going well; the abrupt way he hung up meant the news hadn't been good.

He slapped a hand to the back of his neck and kept his back to her for a moment. She heard his heavy sigh, saw his shoulders sag. "Max," she said quietly, "what's wrong?"

He turned slightly, but not enough so that she could see his face. "Nothing." Then he added, "Everything."

When he faced her, it seemed he'd aged ten years, right before her eyes. She wanted to comfort him, to ease his mind. But a hug didn't seem the medicine he needed right now.

She patted the stool beside her. "C'mere, tell Lily all about it."

For a second there, it looked like he might decline. But soon he was beside her, both elbows leaning on the red-speckled Formica counter. "I've been gone too long," he said, his voice a gruff whisper. "It's time to go back."

Lily's heart ached, just thinking of him being so far away. But hearing that would only add to his stress, so she laid a hand on his forearm.

"I took a leave of absence when Mom broke her leg. Extended it when she had the operation." He heaved a deep breath. "Truth is, I've stayed far longer than she needed me to. She's been up and around for weeks, now."

"Well, maybe she could handle the cash register, but that's about it."

Feeble excuse to keep him here? Lily asked herself. Probably, but if feeble was all she had, she'd use it.

"The other partners are demanding a decision. Soon."

She studied the lines of his strong, masculine profile, and it pained her to see the worry lines beside his mouth, beside his eyes. What had put them there? Dread at the thought of going back...or the thought of staying in Amarillo forever? Lily swallowed hard, terrified of the answer. "How soon?"

He folded his hands on the counter. "They want an answer by the end of the week."

"Saturday? That's awfully fast."

"I wish." He blew a silent whistle. "End of the *business* week." He looked into her eyes. "Tomorrow," he said, and stared straight ahead.

He may as well have said "The End." These few months had been the happiest of her life because Max had been a part of them.

Lily wished she knew what he needed to hear, what he needed her to do right now. Telling him to stay for her sake was out of the question, because this was a guy who'd forced down who knows how many slices of Dutch apple pie rather than hurt his mother's feelings. It would be just like him to quit the firm if she told him the truth—that it would break her heart if he went back to Chicago.

She wouldn't ask that of him. No, if he decided to make Amarillo his home again, it would have to be because *Max* wanted it—not to spare someone's feelings, not to please someone else, but for reasons of his very own.

"Do you...do you have any idea what you'll decide?"

"It's good money. No, *great* money. Nate could go to any college in the world. And the house...it's huge, with a big back yard and a swing set, and a place where he can ride his bike..."

Like her own father, Max was prepared to sacrifice, to suffer for his child. She admired that. Respected it. But she was living proof that no amount of money can buy happiness; she would much rather have seen her dad happy and at peace, than have had all the luxuries his money provided. And she told Max so.

"Nate's a great kid. He'll be happy if you're happy," she said.

Max nodded. "Part of me knows that, of course. And part of me feels he should never have to want for anything."

Customers' forks clinked against their plates as their quiet banter echoed through the diner. The dishwasher clanged pots and pans against the deep stainless-steel sink while Andy's spatula scraped against the grill. It had never been clearer: Life goes on, no matter what. *Oh, Lord,* she prayed, *use me now to bring Max back to You.*

"You'll make the right decision," she said, patting his arm.

He swung to face her. "You're that sure of me, are you?"

Lily read the smile in his eyes. Instinct made her comb through the hair behind his temple, then slide her fingertips across his manly jaw. "Yes, I'm that sure of you."

If he could read her heart, he'd know how far from the truth her answer had been. How could he even consider making a life-altering decision like this without consulting the Almighty!

"Have faith, Max," she blurted. "It'll take you much farther than worry."

His expression turned hard again. "Faith. Don't make me laugh. Name me one reason I should believe in *that*."

"It pulled you through after Melissa's suicide. Got you through Nate's illness and your mom's surgery."

"Faith had nothing to do with it," he insisted. Jabbing a thumb into his chest, Max added, "*I* got me through. God had nothing to do with it…as usual."

The way he tacked on the qualifier reminded Lily he'd once believed—strongly enough to ask God's help, to hope for miracles. "God can't control human beings. I'm sure He wishes He could, but He gave us free will. The best He can hope is we'll make the choices He'd make for us…if He *were* in control of us."

"Oh, don't give me that Bible-thumping, Sunday-go-to-meeting nonsense. I'd have better luck playing with an eight ball than I'd have with prayer."

Obviously, this was neither the time nor the place to try to change his mind about God. But something had better change it, because as much as she loved him, Lily couldn't envision herself spending decades defending her faith! "You have so much to be grateful for!" Lily said, sliding off the stool. "I'd say 'count your blessings' if it didn't sound so trite.'' She grabbed her purse. *I'd say you're acting like a spoiled, immature boy, too*—if she didn't think it would add fuel to his fire.

He looked miserable. But then, why wouldn't he? Max had convinced himself he was on his own, that there was no one he could turn to at times like these. Stubborn as he was, determined as he seemed to be to hold tight to his "If God exists, He doesn't care'' mind-set, she loved him. Lily stood behind him, gave him a little hug and kissed the back of his neck. Lips beside his ear, she whispered, "Count your blessings, Max. You might be surprised how much God has given you.''

Lily didn't give him a chance to argue the point. She was turning out of the parking lot when she wondered if he'd take her advice.

And if he did, would *she* be one of his blessings?

"I've got good news.''

Lily sat on a hay bale and patted the space beside her. "It must be great news, sister dear, the way you're huffing and puffing.''

Cammi sat beside her, biting her bottom lip. "I've just been to see Dr. Anderson,'' she said, and covered her mouth with both hands, trembling with excitement as she waited for Lily to say…

"Dr. Anderson…isn't he an obstetrician?''

Cammi hid behind her hands, peeked between two fingers.

"A baby?'' Lily hugged her. "You and Reid are going to have a baby?''

"Isn't it wonderful?"

After Max's news a few hours earlier, it was more than wonderful. "I'll say." Lily held Cammi at arm's length. "When's the big day?"

"Fourth of July."

"Wow. Talk about a patriotic couple."

"Reid doesn't even know yet. You're so good with ideas, I thought I'd see what you'd come up with— some way I could surprise him."

"I'm flattered to be the first to know," Lily said. She furrowed her brow. "Hmmm...well, you could always wait for the annual pyrotechnics display out at Lake Meredith, tell him during the finale that there's a little firecracker on the way."

"Oh, Lily. Now you're just being silly. Really. Help me come up with something spectacular, something he'll never forget."

She pretended to be insulted. "If he doesn't think a fireworks display is spectacular, maybe I'm wrong," she teased. "Maybe Reid isn't so patriotic, after all."

"I was thinking dinner by candlelight, in the living room, in front of the fireplace. Soft music. A special meal. His favorite dessert." She clapped her hands. "What do you think?"

Cammi positively *glowed* with happy radiance, so much so that it warmed Lily's heart, too. For the moment, she forgot about the possibility that Max might move back to Chicago, that she might never see him again.

"What do I think? I think you wasted your time

coming over here to get my ideas. Sounds like you cooked up the perfect evening all by yourself.''

Cammi nodded. ''Then, it's settled. I'll go to the grocery store on my way back to the Rockin' C.''

''Guess the *C* can stand for 'cradle' now, eh?''

Cammi giggled.

''What *does* that *C* stand for, anyway?''

''Reid inherited the ranch from his adoptive parents, Billy and Martina. He told me once that Billy named the place after an old army buddy, Calvin. He was a rock and roll musician before he joined up. See, Cal loaned him the money for the down payment.''

''Rockin' C. Now I *see*,'' Lily said, laughing.

Cammi frowned suddenly.

''What? A pain? You okay?''

'''Course I am. Are *you* okay? You look like you just lost your best friend.''

''Man. Talk about hitting the old nail on the head.''

''Uh-oh. This is Max-related, isn't it.''

Lily nodded.

Cammi got to her feet and held out her hand. ''Let's go up to the house and talk about it over a cup of tea.''

Over teacups and chocolate chip cookies, Lily filled Cammi in on the state of her relationship with Max. ''...and now he isn't sure if he should go or stay.''

''I remember how awful it was for me when Reid left town to re-up with the rodeo. I feel for ya, kid, honest I do.''

''I've always wondered—if you hadn't followed him, do you think you'd be together today?''

''Nope. He's more stubborn than those bulls he

used to ride. He probably would have sentenced us both to life apart rather than admit how he felt.''

Lily sighed. ''What is it about men? What's so hard about those three little words?''

Cammi grinned. ''Have *you* said 'I love you'?''

She flicked a cookie crumb onto the floor. ''Well, no. I haven't.''

''Why not?''

''Because…because what if he doesn't feel the same way? What if he says—'' Lily assumed the deepest voice she could muster ''—'Sorry, Lil ol' girl, I think you're a great kid and all that, but…''' She rolled her eyes. ''I'd just about die!''

''Have you ever considered that maybe he feels the same way?''

Lily stared into Cammi's bright eyes. ''No. Guess I haven't. But how frustrating is *that?* I mean, how are two people supposed to get together if they're both scared stiff of admitting their feelings!''

''They get together,'' Cammi said, ''because one of them thinks it's worth risking rejection in the hope he or she will hear those three magic words echoed right back at them.''

Lily took a sip of tea, then grinned. ''I can't wait 'til I'm as old and wise as you.''

''Neither can I,'' Cammi teased. She got up and grabbed her purse from where she'd hung it on the chair back. ''Well, I'm off to the store.'' She checked items off an imaginary list, written on her palm. ''One romantic evening, one joyful husband, one spectacular celebration…''

Walking beside her to the back door, Lily added, "Can't wait 'til I'm as happy as you are, either."

Cammi hugged her tight. "Aw, Lil...that day will come. I know it will. Where's your faith?"

Lily waved as her sister headed toward her car. Ironic, she thought, that Cammi would pose that particular question. Especially considering the lecture she'd laid on Max a few hours earlier.

"'Judge not lest ye be judged,'" she quoted, because Cammi was right. If she believed things would work out between her and Max, they would.

Right?

Common sense prevailed: They'd work out if God saw it as part of His plan.

Let it be part of Your plan! Lily prayed.

"Hardly seems fair," Georgia said when Max broke the news to her that day. "I mean, you're not taking more than your share of the profits, right?"

Max shook his head. "No, but the partners have had to divide my clients among them. They want full percentages if things are going to stay this way."

"What did you tell them?"

"The truth," he said.

"Which is?"

"I don't know."

His mother sighed. "Seems a shame for you to go back to that rat race. You've seemed so calm and rested here." She glanced over at her grandson, who was filling a paint-by-numbers canvas with primary colors as Robert looked on. "And Nate took to Amarillo like a born Texan!"

"I know, I know."

She waved Robert over. "Well, here's something that might make your decision a little easier." Once her fiancé joined her in the booth, Georgia said, "We've decided to retire after we get married."

That surprised Max, and he said so.

"There's a big wide wonderful world out there," his future stepfather said, "and we've both worked so hard, we've only seen a small slice of it. And we want to see it, together."

His mother had worked hard all her life. Max couldn't remember her ever taking more than a day or two away from the diner. "What about this place?" he asked. "Andy's a great guy, a terrific fry cook, but I've seen him make change. You don't want him keeping the books."

"You're right. He means well, but his math skills sure leave a lot to be desired." Georgia leaned forward, waved Max closer. "But I have it all figured out," she whispered. "Piece of cake."

"Easy as pie," Robert added.

"Simple as—"

Hands up in mock surrender, Max laughed. "Okay, okay. I get it. So out with it, already. What's this idea of yours?"

Robert slid a fat brown envelope from his inside jacket pocket. "Open it."

The envelope contained the deed to Georgia's Diner, a topographical map of the lot, a license to operate an Amarillo business, and an inventory of the restaurant's equipment. Max was more than happy to provide them with a little free tax advice. He leafed through the documents and then, folding them up again, nodded. "Everything appears to be in order." He held out the folder. "You planning to hire a live-in manager?"

Georgia and Robert exchanged a glance. "Sort of," she said without taking the envelope.

Max donned his most professional pose—elbows on the table, hands clasped atop the paperwork. "You aren't planning to leave on your world tour tomorrow, so it isn't like there's any big rush. You have plenty of time to find someone trustworthy to run the place while you're gone." Grinning, he shrugged. "Who knows? You might miss the place."

Georgia wrapped a hand around her beau's arm. "Not a chance. I've given this place my all. Rarely spent a dime of my tip money, put most of the profits back into the business."

Max said, "Which is why it's the busiest eatery in town."

"Which is *also* why I'm the tiredest diner owner in town. I have some zip in my step...or soon will, thanks to ol' Robert, here, so—"

"Hey," the man teased, "who you callin' old?"

"I want to enjoy what's left of my life. No more getting up at 3:00 a.m. to drive to the markets for vegetables and meats. No more baking pies 'til all hours of the night. No more smiling when some trucker complains that his burger wasn't cooked enough...or that it was overcooked. No more soups to stir, or chili pots to scrub."

"Mom," Max said, blanketing her hands with his, "no one is saying you don't deserve some freedom from this place. You've been a slave to it most of your life!''

He'd seen expressions of anger, weariness, joy and disgust on her face, but Max had never seen *that* look before. She continued to sit there, blinking and silent, refusing to take back the diner's paperwork.

When Georgia looked down, turned her engagement ring around and around, Max thought he'd figured it out.

"Mom, it's been in your family since Great-Grandma Georgia first moved to Amarillo. You can't be seriously considering selling the place...."

Her head snapped up. "'Course not," she said. "I want you to have it. Lock, stock and griddle brick."

Max laughed nervously. "Me? You're kidding, right?"

He glanced from Georgia's serious face to Robert's and back again. "You're *not* kidding." The documents suddenly seemed too hot to touch, so he sat back and crossed both arms over his chest.

"Even if I was interested, I can't afford it right now. Everything I have is tied up in the house in Chicago, in the firm. It'd take weeks to liquidate."

"Maxwell Sheridan, don't you insult your mama that way! I wouldn't dream of taking a dime from you. Why, you wouldn't let me pay a penny of your college tuition. And when you went into that business out there in Chicago, you wouldn't let me help you."

She turned to Robert. "Do you realize that every time things got tough around here, money-wise, this boy bailed me out? Why, there were times I'd have gone belly-up for sure if he hadn't come to the rescue.''

She faced Max again. "And you refused to let me pay those loans back. You've bought and paid for this place twice over, way I see it!''

"Mom…''

"Son, you love this place every bit as much as I do. You'd hate seeing it go to strangers.''

She was right on both counts. "But, Mom, I'm a lousy cook, and—''

"Andy has agreed to stay on.''

Max frowned. "—and I'm clumsy as they come. I don't think I've ever delivered a meal without spilling something.''

"Vera will stay, and so will Betty. They're two of the finest waitresses in all of Texas.'' Georgia winked. "I oughta know, I trained 'em myself!''

True again. But he didn't say so.

"Think of yourself as the overseer,'' Robert suggested. "Someone who balances the books, orders the food, counts the cash.''

Georgia nodded. "Right! And you wouldn't even have to set foot in the kitchen if you didn't want to.'' She hesitated. "'Til the health department did its annual inspection, that is.'' Another pause. "And of course you'd pass, 'cause, like I said, I trained Betty and Vera my very own self.''

It was definitely something to think about. Because he didn't relish the idea of going back to Chicago, picking up where he'd left off, even if the money he earned out there did guarantee Nate could attend the Ivy League college of his choice.

His mother had been right about something else, too: he *had* felt good, real good, since coming home. And Nate had taken to the place like a fish to water.

Then there was the matter of Lily....

"Like you said," Robert said, "we're not going anywhere tomorrow, or even the next day. Take some time, bounce the idea around a bit."

Max didn't have time; he had promised Donald Wilkes he'd have an answer by tomorrow. But he nodded anyway. "I'll give it some thought." Then he added, "When do you need to know?"

Georgia looked suddenly guilty, like a little girl caught with her fingers in the cookie jar. "Just take your time, son."

But she hadn't meant a word of it; the tension in her voice told Max she had something up her sleeve. If experience hadn't long ago taught him it would be a waste of time and energy to ask *what,* he'd nag it out of her.

Still, she hadn't had to write it on the menu board: they needed to know ASAP.

So now he faced *two* deadlines. Three, if he counted the self-imposed restriction he'd put on himself where his future with Lily was concerned.

"Pray on it, son," Georgia said, patting his hand. "The Good Lord will let you know what's best for you and Nate."

Not a chance, he thought, echoing his mom's earlier quote. "Mind if I take these with me?" he asked, pointing to the papers.

"If you make the right choice, they're yours."

Georgia slid them to the edge of the table. "So be my guest."

"I'm going up to bed now," he said, bussing her cheek. And reaching across her, he shook Robert's hand. "Drive safe goin' home."

He was halfway up the back stairs when he heard his mother holler, "Pray on it, son!"

Max took a deep breath. "Okay, Mom." Maybe prayer was his only way out.

It never had worked before, no reason to believe it would work now.

But he was pretty much out of options...so what could it hurt?

Max tossed and turned until his sheets were in a knot. Since it was obvious sleep would elude him, he got up and headed for the living room.

He stood for a long time, just looking around at the tables and chairs, at flea-market paintings on the walls, at the place he'd called home as a boy, as a young man.

This was a good room, filled with plain colors and plainer furnishings, where on Sunday mornings his father sat in the big easy chair, giving the newspaper a hearty *flap* every time he turned a page. "You'll put me in the loony bin with your paper-snapping," his mother would say.

But it hadn't been a scolding, not really; their eyes would meet, and his dad's wry grin and his mom's merry wink were proof that, different as they are, man and woman could share...life.

Shortly after her husband's death, Georgia began

turning on his desk lamp every night before going to bed. "He needs the light to guide him," she'd say as she twisted the tiny brass button on its base 'til one *click* echoed in the quiet night. "Not much light, just enough, so he won't trip or stub his toe on his way to our room." She wound his pocket watch every night, too, and gently laid it atop the blotter, arranging the fob in an *S* pattern...*S* for Steven. Then her fingertips would graze the top rung of his desk chair, lingering.

Max was grateful for having grown up in a house filled with love like that. It had surrounded him as a boy, like warm tidal waters and fresh, sunny air. No wonder it had been so easy to recognize love when he saw it for himself.

His mother didn't look at her new fiancé in quite the same way she'd looked at Max's dad. But then, Robert probably didn't look at Georgia as he'd looked at his first wife, either. They'd met each other in time, and that was all that mattered. Max was grateful for that, too.

He heard Nate in the next room, muttering in his sleep. Max closed his eyes and reveled in the sound. He'd almost lost the boy, twice. He was thankful that he'd been an eyewitness to back-to-back miracles, and now his one and only son grew more healthy and robust with each passing day.

Lily had been right...he had needed to count his blessings.

He sat on the hard wooden chair that matched his father's desk and adjusted the lamp's goose-neck until its dim beam illuminated the documents his mother had given him. Should he run the diner so it could remain in the family? Or go back to Chicago, where a big house and a corner office in a fancy skyscraper waited for him?

The steady *tick-tick-tick* of his dad's pocket watch seemed to be telling him, *"Stay, stay, stay…"*

Max padded into the kitchen on socked feet, turned on the flame under the teakettle. It was all the light he needed to see his favorite cup, resting upside down in the drainboard. When the water was hot, he'd make himself some hot chocolate. Wouldn't be as tasty as the stuff Lily whipped up, but maybe it would make him drowsy.

He needed a good night's sleep, because tomorrow, first thing, he'd book a flight to the O'Hare airport, take a cab to Wilkes Towers and start the "I'm outta here" ball rolling. Max wasn't sure exactly when he'd made the decision. He only knew that he couldn't go back to that life, or that world. Not when everything he'd ever wanted was already here.

He'd keep things to himself for a while, at least until his house was on the market and he'd discussed a fair and reasonable settlement with the Wilkes partners.

It felt good, knowing he was home again—home to stay. So good that he turned off the teapot before the water even began to simmer. What did he need with store-bought cocoa when he'd found the girl who would make it for him from scratch!

Max tidied his sheets and climbed back into bed. On his back, with fingers linked behind his neck, he stared at the ceiling. Was God really up there, someplace far beyond his boyhood toys in the attic and abandoned birds' nests still tucked among the eaves? Could He truly hear the voices of nondescript humans calling through the clouds and the stars for help from on high? And if He heard, why had He so often turned a deaf ear to *this* human? Max wondered.

He remembered Lily's words in the car that day, when Nate asked a similar question. ''Maybe He isn't saying yes or no,'' she'd said. ''Maybe He's saying 'wait.'''

Wait.

The silence was interrupted only by the tire-*hiss* of the occasional passing car. It was easy to wait, when the world was at rest, when life was so quiet. Not so easy in the bright light of day. At least, not without practice.

He'd waited a lifetime for Lily. He could wait a few more days, until he could turn the last page on the Chicago chapter of his life.

Chapter Ten

"Hey, Lil...I have to go to Chicago. Sure would be nice if you could come, too—"

Lily listened to the message three times before throwing her purse across the room. What had cut off the end of his message?

She dialed the diner, hoping Georgia would be there.

"Geor-gia's," the redhead sang into the phone.

"Hi, Georgia. It's Lily."

"Howdy, kiddo!"

"How's the leg?"

"Still attached, last time I checked." She chuckled. "Robert says if I stick with my physical therapy, I might be able to throw this nasty cane away by Valentine's Day."

"That's wonderful news. I'll keep you on my prayer list. Make sure you keep doing your exercises."

Another chuckle. "Thanks. I think." Georgia paused. "So what can I do for you, kiddo?"

"When I got back from Lake Meredith, there was a strange message from Max on my answering machine. I was just wondering if—"

"What were you doing up there *this* time?"

"Oh, some goofy hikers left a bunch of twine at their campsite, and a spike buck got tangled in it. Ended up pinned to a tree trunk. Boy Scouts troop leader called me from his cell phone."

Georgia clucked her tongue. "Those addle-brained fools. Is the li'l guy all right?"

"Will be, once his cuts and scrapes heal. I just got him settled in a stall."

"So, about this message from Max…"

"He said he was on his way to Chicago." Lily's heart pounded at the thought. "When did he leave, exactly?"

"Day before yesterday. But don't worry, he'll be back."

"He will?"

"Has to. He left Nate with me." Georgia's laughter filtered through the phone line.

"You wouldn't have his phone number handy, would you?"

"Home, office, fax or cell?" Georgia asked.

"I'll try all of them." Her hand trembled as she wrote down the numbers Georgia dictated. "Just one more question. Is he…is he coming back for good?"

"I sure hope so."

Georgia didn't sound as jovial, as sure of herself,

suddenly, and it made Lily's blood run cold. "Well, thanks. Take care of yourself."

If the woman had more to say, Lily didn't hear it. Dazed by the news that Max had left town, she hung up without another word.

Suddenly, she was reminded of her conversation with Cammi the other day. Her sister had followed Reid all the way to Montana or Idaho or...Lily couldn't remember where. The only thing that really mattered was that the trip had a happy ending— Cammi and Reid wound up together.

And they were married.

And now they were going to have a baby.

Lily raced up the stairs, dialing Cammi's number as she went. "Hey, can you do me a huge favor?" she asked when her sister answered the phone.

"If I can, 'course I will."

"I'll need you to feed the animals for a couple of days. Do you think Reid will mind helping?"

"I've done it all before. I don't need his help."

"I just brought home a spike buck. Nothing serious wrong with him, but he's strong as a bull elephant. Reid will need to hold him while you change the bandage on his leg."

"What happened to him?"

"Long story. Mind if I tell you when I get back?"

"Mind telling me where you're going?"

"Chicago."

"Ah, I should have known." Cammi sighed. "When are you leaving?"

"I'm packing as we speak," she said, throwing her

suitcase onto the bed. "Hopefully, I can get a flight out of Amarillo International today."

"I'll pray that you get your flight, that you arrive safely, that you find that knucklehead when you get there...and drag him home!"

"Thanks, Cam. I owe you big time for this one."

"Tell me something I don't know," Cammi said, snickering.

Lily put jeans and sweaters, a business suit and a simple black dress into the suitcase as she asked how Cammi was feeling. She prayed her sister wouldn't miscarry this child, as she had her last. Satisfied Cammi was doing well, Lily hung up and ran downstairs to write her father a note: "Going to Chicago. Explain later. Call you when I get there. Take care! All my love, Lily."

All the way to the airport, she prayed.

Prayed there'd be a seat for her on a standby flight, that she wouldn't get lost in the maze of terminals that made up Chicago's O'Hare.

Prayed she'd be able to find her way to a hotel in the city, that there'd be a room available.

Because wasn't Chicago known as "Convention City"?

Or was that New York?

Lily prayed that once she got hold of Max, he'd sound genuinely happy to hear from her.

But most of all, she prayed he wouldn't tell her he intended to stay in Chicago permanently.

Because if he said that, Lily would have to pray for the strength to return to Amarillo without him.

* * *

Lily sat on the edge of her hotel room bed and used her cell phone to call Max's. On the third ring, she began rehearsing what she'd record on his voice mail; on the fourth, he said, "Sheridan."

"Max. Hi. It's Lily."

"Hey, there! Good to hear from you. Did you get my message?"

"Part of it. Something cut you off after your invitation to Chicago."

"No way. Man. Well, no wonder you never called me back, then."

"That's only half the reason. I had an emergency."

"Everybody's okay back there, I hope."

She smiled. How like him to worry about the people she loved. "Everyone's fine. It was an animal rescue kind of thing. I was at Lake Meredith all weekend. And like a ninny, I forgot my cell phone."

"So, how are ya?" he asked.

"Cold." And it was true. "I could probably have lived my entire life without knowing why they call Chicago the Windy City. I don't know how people stand it!"

"Whoa. You're in town?"

Maybe she shouldn't have come. Maybe politeness had made him invite her. *Maybe you should answer his question.* "Yes. I'm staying at the Sheraton Towers."

"No kidding? When did you get here?"

"About an hour ago."

"You here 'cause of my message?"

Why else would she have traveled nearly nine hundred miles, enduring a luggage search and being frisked at both ends of the line! "I was just curious to see how the other half lives."

Max laughed. "You're in for a major disappointment, then. I'm glad you decided to come, though, whatever the reason."

He was the one and only reason!

"Say...have you had anything to eat yet?"

"Not since this morning."

"I have a few loose ends to tie up here. How 'bout when I'm finished, I pick you up and buy you some dinner?"

"Sounds great. What time should I be ready?"

"I'll give you a call as soon as I finish up. What's your room number?"

She told him, then hung up, immediately wishing she'd asked what kind of dinner he had in mind. Because Lily would hate to show up in blue jeans if he had something fancier in mind—

The phone interrupted her reverie.

"Hey, Lil," he said when she answered. "How would you feel about joining me for dinner at one of the partners' homes? The firm's senior partner is throwing a shindig to show off his new house. Mansion is more like it," he said, laughing. "The thing has ten bedrooms, eight bathrooms and five fireplaces! We'll leave there with full bellies, 'cause his wife Brandy really knows how to put on a banquet!"

Brandy? Lily had a feeling she was going to put the proverbial bull in a china shop to shame. Already, her hands had begun to shake. "Sure. Why not?"

She agreed to meet him in the lobby, seven o'clock sharp. The alarm on her night table said 3:04 p.m.

More than enough time for a nap before she showered and dressed for the…*banquet*. Lily opened her suitcase and had started putting clothes on hangers when the phone rang again.

"Make it six," Max said. "I want to show you my office before we head over to Donald's house."

He sounded so businesslike, so matter-of-fact. Maybe the icy temperatures had that effect on his vocal cords. Had he missed her as much as she'd missed him? Had he thought about her nonstop, dreamed about her, pictured her during idle moments?

"Lily?"

"Yes?"

"Thought we'd been disconnected for a minute there. So, what do you say? Okay if we meet at six instead of seven?"

"Sure," she said again. "Why not?"

This time when the call ended, Lily lay down on the thick quilt covering the massive bed. How would she wear her hair? Was the little black dress she'd brought elegant enough for a banquet in a mansion? Max would be introducing her to the other partners in his accounting firm. Because he intended to ask her to stay here with him? Or simply because he didn't want to attend the function alone?

The clock said 3:45 p.m. now. She'd left the house at eight in the morning, managed to snag a seat on a standby direct flight from the Amarillo airport to O'Hare. Stretching, Lily yawned. "Guess you'll find out soon enough," she said, closing her eyes.

From Max's office, tucked in a corner on the penthouse floor of one of the city's tallest skyscrapers,

Lily could see most of Chicago. She didn't know much about commercial real estate, but she knew the price rose with the elevator.

"I'm impressed," she said.

"Don't be. I'm not."

There it was again—that incredible nonchalance that had led her to believe the firm was made up of a couple of college buddies, that maybe they'd rented the ground floor of a house-turned-office on a busy side street.

"You have every right to be proud of what you've accomplished," she insisted, running a fingertip along the arm of his desk chair. Its buttery brown leather matched the sofa and love seat that faced one another along a mahogany wall lined with hardcover books.

"Didn't say I wasn't proud." He shrugged and pocketed his hands. "I'm just not impressed."

"That's okay. I'm impressed enough for the both of us."

He sat in the enormous chair and pulled out a desk drawer. "Mind waiting while I make a quick call to Nate?"

"Take your time," she said, taking a seat in one of the beige upholstered wing chairs facing his desk. "Tell him I said hi."

She watched him chat with his son, laughing and nodding in response to something the boy had said. If Max didn't love that kid with everything in him, Lily thought, he'd missed his calling as an actor. He seemed to have infinite patience with Nate, whether the boy was recounting a movie he'd just seen, word for word, or singing a song he'd just learned.

"I miss you, too, kiddo. Kiss Gramma good-night for me." He paused, listening, and Lily knew even before he responded what Nate had said, for Max's face lit up brighter than the Christmas tree in Rockefeller Center.

"I love you, too. I'll call you tomorrow, okay?"

"He's some kid," she said when he hung up.

Max stared at the phone for a moment. "You can say that again." He met her eyes. "I want you to know, I took your advice."

Brows raised, she asked, "What advice?"

Max stood, shoved the chair under the desk. "You were right. I have plenty to be thankful for."

She got to her feet, too, and followed him to the massive double doors.

"You gave me a lot to think about, which is why I'm here in Chicago. Had some tough decisions to make, and your 'count your blessings' advice made me decide to—"

The many-buttoned black phone on his desk buzzed, cutting off the rest of his sentence.

His shiny shoes thudded softly as he crossed the Persian carpeted floor. "Sheridan," he said into the mouthpiece. He listened a moment, then said, "Why don't you just take a cab?" Another moment of silence. "All right. I'll be there in—" he checked his watch "—give us fifteen minutes. What? Oh, 'us.'" He glanced at Lily. "Nobody you'd know. Friend of mine from Amarillo."

Whoever was on the other end of that call made

him nervous. Max ran a hand through his hair even before he hung up. And when he met her eyes this time, she got the feeling Max wasn't really seeing her at all.

"You ready?" he said, opening the door.

Lily nodded and stepped into the enormous, well-appointed waiting suite. Here, as in his office, the furnishings were rich in texture, subtle in color. Wood tones and earthy hues were in abundance, from the recessed light fixtures in the ceiling to the plush carpeting underfoot.

Max Sheridan was a wealthy man, perhaps more so than her father. And like her dad, he'd never gloated or boasted about it. In fact, to look at him, to talk to him, a person would think he was barely making ends meet!

He walked ahead to push the elevator button. "Ritzy digs, eh?" he teased. "Rent around here is sky-high, so I talked the guys into buying the space. Best investment we ever made."

She couldn't help but notice that he held his head higher here, spoke with a quiet authority that hadn't been necessary back in Amarillo. There, he'd donned blue jeans and cotton shirts; here, he wore a suit that screamed "made in Italy!"

"It's a beautiful office," she said.

As the brass-doored elevator hissed shut, Max jutted out his chin and folded his hands behind his back. "It'll do."

If he could be that casual about opulence like this, what must his home look like!

"If we get out of Wilkes's early enough, maybe

I'll drive you over to my house—see what you think of the place.''

In the months since his return to Texas, Lily had learned he'd been blessed with many gifts. 'Til now, she hadn't realized mind reading was one of them.

But wait… Why would he care what she thought of his house—unless he planned to ask her to share it with him?

He'd lived there with his wife. In fact, Melissa had died at that address. Lily seemed to be moving farther and farther from her ''rose-covered cottage'' dream.…

''Have I told you that you look gorgeous tonight?''

Lily blushed. ''Only about a dozen times.''

''Yep,'' he said in his thickest Texas drawl. ''Y'clean up purty good…fer a li'l farm girl.''

Wink or no wink, his teasing comment made Lily bristle. No one had ever called her a *farm girl,* not even in jest. She'd been born and bred a rancher's daughter, and grew up to be proud of it!

''It's pretty brisk out there,'' he said once the elevator reached the lobby. ''Why don't you wait here while I bring my car around?''

''Your car?''

He chuckled. ''Let me guess…you thought because of the fancy-schmancy office, I have a chauffeured limousine waiting at the curb?'' An out-and-out laugh this time. ''Sweetheart, you think far too highly of me!''

Lily hid her frustration behind a pleasant smile. But while he was out getting the car, she couldn't help but think he was a different Max out here. "I mean, really… *'sweetheart'*?"

"What's that, ma'am?" the doorman said.

"Don't mind me," she told him with an exaggerated southern accent. "I'm just a crazy little farmer from Texas who doesn't know what to make of the tall buildings y'all have out here!"

The man tipped his black-billed hat and went back to standing by the door.

He probably believes you, she thought.

Before she knew it, the huge thick-glass door swung open. "Your ride is here, ma'am," said the uniformed gent.

"Why, thank y'all," she said, smiling her biggest, brightest smile. "Y'all just have the *nicest* manners 'roun' these parts. Wait 'til I git home an' tell mah daddy." She leaned close to whisper, "Here he was, thinkin' all you big-city folk were mean an' nasty. Ain't he gonna be surprised!"

Max opened the passenger door of a low-slung silver convertible. The doorman handed Lily off as if he were only too glad to be getting rid of her. Not that she blamed him. It hadn't been fair to make him pay for Max's remark.

She saw Max tuck paper money into his gloved hand and hoped it had been a generous tip. *The man earned it tonight,* she thought, grinning slightly.

Lily continued with the overdone drawl. "This is a right-fine car you've got yourself here, if I do say so myself."

He cut her a quick, puzzled glance. "Uh…thanks."

''Bet this baby ain't no gas guzzler. Bet she parks like a dream, too, don't she?''

Max braked at a red light. ''Lily, what…?'' His confused expression smoothed to one of comprehension. ''Okay, I get it. You took offense at that 'farm girl' reference, didn't you?''

She stiffened. ''Of course not. Don't be silly.''

''Seems to me *you're* the one being silly. You should know I'd never say anything to deliberately hurt your feelings or insult you. If I did, I'm sorry.''

Lily felt like a selfish, spoiled brat. She sighed. ''Let's just blame it on the long trip. I really hate to fly these days.''

He patted her hand. ''Okay…''

He'd left his sentence unfinished. Curiosity ate at her until she said, ''Okay *what?*''

''Okay, Silly Lily.''

She had to hand it to him. Max sure knew how to calm a tense moment. But then, he'd had four years of practice, thanks to Nate. The knowledge didn't do much to erase her mind-set.

He fiddled with the radio dials, stuffed a couple of CDs into the changer, adjusted the knobs on the dash. It wasn't until Max used his coat sleeve to dust the top of the steering column that Lily thought he was taking tidiness a bit too far.

Yes, he was definitely different out here. In Amarillo, he drove with the windows down and didn't even seem to notice how much dust and grit accumulated on the car's interior! But then, Georgia's old boat probably hadn't cost one-tenth what Max had paid for *this* piece of machinery. And obviously, he was very pleased and proud of his purchase.

It was a nice car, to be sure. But really, Lily thought as he used his sleeve again, this time to buff the steering wheel, it's *a car!*

He pulled into a driveway, put the sports car into "park" and tooted the horn.

"Sounds like a roadrunner," she teased.

"Which is precisely why I bought it," he shot back, grinning. "Reminds me of home."

He climbed out of the car and walked around to the passenger side as a tall, leggy blonde sashayed toward them.

Chapter Eleven

She had the walk of a runway model, the wave of a British royal. Max was out of the car in a heartbeat, taking her elbow and escorting her to the passenger door. *This* was the partner Max had agreed to drive to the banquet? Lily's heart all but ceased beating.

"Lily London, this is Susan Fisher. Lily and I go way back."

"So you said on the phone…an old Texas chum." She laughed.

"I hate to make you stand in the cold, Lil," Max said, "but would you mind, just long enough for Susan, here, to climb in."

The blonde tucked her chin into her neck. "You have *got* to be kidding! No way these legs of mine would fit back there!" As if to prove it, she stuck one out for Max and Lily to see. She looked imploringly at Lily. "You have shorter legs." And wrinkling her nose, she added, "Would you mind terribly much if I rode up front?"

Lily got out of the car, then got right back in and settled down in the back.

"Thanks," Susan said, taking Lily's place. "You're a doll." She struggled with the seat belt for a moment, then grunted with frustration. "Maxie, be a dear and fasten it for me, will you?" Over her shoulder she added for Lily's benefit, "This thing has *always* given me fits!"

Max leaned in, headfirst, and snapped the buckle into place. "All tucked in?"

When she nodded, he closed the door.

"Doll," indeed, Lily grumbled to herself. It was pretty apparent by things Susan had said that she and Max were more than business associates. But how much more? And for how long? If they were more than friends, why had he invited Lily here?

Maybe what he'd said on the answering machine had only *sounded* like an invitation. Maybe the half of the message that she hadn't received said something entirely different.

"You okay back there?" Max asked her, downshifting.

"Fine and dandy."

Susan laid a long-taloned hand atop his. "Isn't she the cutest little thing?"

"Yeah," he said. "Cute."

Lily didn't know what to make of his tone. She knew this: Coming to Chicago had been a mistake. A *big* mistake.

Well, she told herself, *you're in it up to your earlobes now.* What choice did she have but to go along for the ride, literally and figuratively?

As they headed for the Wilkes's mansion, Susan told Max about the cellist who'd played a solo at the symphony the night before, about the way she'd cried at the end of the ballet last week. She'd heard the most talented new tenor singing at the opera. Her techno-stock had risen in value by *two whole points!* And the latest client to sign on with the firm was sure to send their profits through the roof this year. "But really, Max," Susan said, one long, red fingernail drawing circles on the back of his hand, "if it hadn't been for your securing the Vanemier account, I don't know where we'd be. Why, the Vanemiers recommended so many of their contemporaries that…"

Lily put her hands over her ears. If she had to listen to another word of this drivel, her head might just explode.

"You sure you're okay back there?"

She met Max's eyes in the rearview mirror and quickly put her hands in her lap. "Yup. Right as rain."

"Rain…that reminds me," Susan said, "I'm going to my cabin in Wisconsin this weekend, and the weather man says it's going to be great ski weather. Care to join me?"

"Nah. Thanks, though."

"But, Maxie, you love to ski!"

"I have to pass."

"Remember last time we went skiing? When you tried the 'expert' slope? Oh, if only I had a picture of your face when you came down that hill." Susan threw her head back and laughed.

Everything about her was sultry, from her deep,

husky voice to her shapely legs to her waist-long golden hair. No wonder Max was attracted to her.

Lily winced.

Evidently, she'd taken the quiet moments she and Max had experienced, the warm kisses, the caring conversation, far more seriously than he had. He'd been right to call her Silly Lily earlier, but not because she'd teased a doorman! It had been absurd to read so much into what he'd said, into what they'd shared.

Correction: into what she'd *thought* they shared.

"Have you fallen asleep back there?" Susan asked. "I haven't heard a peep out of you since we left my house."

If only sleep *could* rescue her from this moment! "Oh, I'm awake. Just mesmerized by the scintillating conversation going on up there."

It was too dark to read Max's eyes in the rearview mirror. But something told Lily that her remark had not amused him. *Tough beans, Maxie,* Lily thought. She knew exactly what Cammi would say to that: "Tough beans? Such language!" The thought made her smile. Which reminded her that, no matter what happened between her and Max—between Max and Susan—Lily would always have her family to love and protect her.

The mention of family made her think of Nate. Had Susan met the boy? And if she had, had she liked him? "Say, *Maxie,*" Lily said over the seat, "when's Nate's bedtime? Eight o'clock, right?"

Max nodded. "Uh-huh."

"He'd probably love it if you called, sang him a lullaby over the phone."

"A squeaking door hinge can hold a tune better than I can."

"Oh, I dunno," Lily insisted. "I've heard you humming around the diner. You're not so bad."

"Diner?"

Susan's voice wasn't so honeyed now, Lily noted.

"Would anybody mind if I made a quick stop at my place?" he said quickly. "I seem to have forgotten my wallet."

Nice save, Max, Lily thought. But "I don't mind" is what she said.

"We'll be late," Susan protested. "You know how Donald hates tardiness."

"We'll make it on time. My house is five minutes from the Wilkes's."

Max lived that close to a neighborhood full of mansions? What other things would she learn about him during this short visit to Illinois?

"Max," Susan said dully, "why must you always push the envelope? Honestly, sometimes I don't know what to think of you."

What would she think of Max the short-order cook, Lily wondered, or Max the waiter? Would she draw pictures on the backs of his hands if she'd seen them buried deep in a tub of sudsy water, washing greasy dishes? How would she feel about Max the doting son, who'd carried his injured mother up and down the stairs for weeks, who'd lovingly changed the dressing on her incision every morning? And what of the Max who'd nearly worn the speckles off the hospital's linoleum, pacing while his little boy was in surgery? Would she find his paternal concern attractive?

Something told Lily that Susan had no idea such a Max existed.

The car stopped in front of his house. "I'll leave the car running," he said, opening the driver's door. "Won't be but a minute."

"Mind if I use your little girls' room, as long as we're here?" Lily asked. Seeing inside the place would tell her still more about him. And she wanted to learn every detail, no matter how small.

He huffed a bit, then shoved his seat forward, extending a hand to help her out of the car. Lily pretended not to see it. No sense stirring up memories of times when he'd sandwiched her hands between his own; that would only remind her of happier moments.

"You know, I think I might just join you," Susan said. "My nose could use a little powdering."

Max walked ahead to unlock the door.

"Maybe you can give me a tour, Susan."

"Tour?" Susan stopped suddenly, as though someone had nailed her shoes to the redbrick driveway. "I...well..." She brightened, gathering her composure. "Of course. I'd be happy to."

Without knowing it, she'd given Lily the answer to a question she hadn't even asked: Susan had never been to Max's house. Lily's heartbeat doubled with relief.

He flipped a switch in the foyer, ushered his guests inside. "Powder room is the third door on your left, down that hall, there," he told Lily. And to Susan he said, "Wallet's on the dresser. Be down in no time. If you don't want to wait for the powder room, there's another bathroom one floor down, end of the hall."

Lily and Susan stood side by side, watching as he took the stairs two at a time. They glanced around, taking in the polished hardwood floor, the curved staircase with its mahogany railing, the enormous oil paintings hanging on the walls of the two-storied room. A grandfather clock chimed in the distance, counting out the seven o'clock hour.

"Uh-oh," Lily said. "'We're late, we're late…'"

Surprisingly, Susan laughed. "'…for a very important date,'" she finished.

Okay, so the big blonde wasn't *all* bad. Her only flaw, really, was a colossal interest in Max, and Lily could hardly blame her for that.

They walked through the darkened, quiet rooms, peering into doorways, looking around corners. It was a big house, bigger than he'd made it sound. Tastefully furnished with overstuffed sofas and chairs upholstered in muted plaids and elegant stripes. Had Melissa done the decorating? Or had Max had the place done over after the suicide, to hurry the healing along?

"So, have you two had your fill yet?"

Susan squealed and Lily gasped.

"Maxie! You scared me out of ten years of my life."

"Don't give it another thought," Lily told her. "From what I hear, those last ten years are the hardest, anyway."

Again, Susan laughed at Lily's joke. If not for their common interest in Max, maybe they could be friends....

The instant her shock at his sudden appearance wore off, Susan struck a pose: one high heel in front of the other, knee bent and hip thrust out slightly, right shoulder a tad higher than the left, head tilted *just* enough.

On second thought, Lily admitted, maybe they couldn't be friends, after all. "Beautiful house, Max," Lily said. "Your decorator has exquisite taste."

Leading them back to the foyer, he laughed. "Decorator?"

Susan lowered her head and looked up at him through mascara-rimmed eyes. "Don't tell me you did this all by yourself?"

He opened the front door. "Okay, I won't tell you."

Lily wasn't surprised. He had a certain masculine sensitivity about him, an eye for detail. She gave him a playful shot to the arm on her way by. "Nice job, pal. I'm impressed. Again."

"Don't be impressed. I'm not."

The look he gave her, when he said it, was reminiscent of those marvelous, magical moments on her front porch on Thanksgiving Day.

But Lily couldn't afford to put any stock in her memories.

During dinner, Lily laughed quietly at Donald Wilkes's knock-knock jokes. But her attention wasn't on the senior partner or his corny riddles, his elegant silk gabardine suit or his thousand-dollar-per-place-setting china. Fingers drumming lightly on the base of an intricately carved crystal goblet, she watched from the corner of her eye the couple who'd been seated directly across from her.

Susan had gradually slid her dinnerware nearer to Max's, allowing her to sit closer, to touch his hand each time she apologized for bumping his elbow or leaning into his shoulder. Much to Lily's dismay, Max didn't seem to mind a bit. If he'd figured out Susan's little scheme, it sure didn't show on his face. In fact, it looked to her as if he was flattered by the blonde's blatant flirtations!

They seemed to have much in common, much more than just their work. There was opera and ballet, the symphony, stocks and bonds... But Susan didn't seem the type who'd warm to children. Didn't look like the kind of woman Nate could relate to.

He'd lived in that quiescently dignified house for years, yet hadn't invited Susan to it. If they had so much in common, if he thought so highly of her, why hadn't she been a guest before?

"Who hasn't seen the house?" Wilkes asked. He picked up his wineglass, sloshing a bit of the red stuff on the white linen tablecloth. "Follow me, people, and we'll take the grand tour!"

"Donald," his wife scolded, "look what you're doing!"

He blotted the stain with a matching napkin. "Not to worry, darling. I'll buy you a new one. I'll buy you *ten* new ones!" His bawdy laughter bounced off the faux-suede painted walls. "Thanks to Sheridan, here, we'll have plenty of money come bonus time." He raised his glass. "A toast to Maxwell, for bringing us the biggest account in all of the Midwest!"

Quiet murmurs of appreciation and a smattering of applause resounded in the room. But no one patted him on the back, no one shook his hand, Lily noticed. What a difference between this crowd and her father's cronies!

One by one, the guests followed Donald and his wife for the "grand tour." Max, however, lingered in the library. "Been there, done that," he explained when Susan waved at him to come along. "Bought the T-shirt and outgrew it."

"C'mon, Lily," Donald slurred, grabbing her elbow. "Lesh go shee the resht of my place. I tol' the architect to make a copy of the stairs in *Gone with the Wind*," he said. "Whaddaya think? Doesh it look like Scarlett's staircase?"

The last thing Lily heard before he guided her toward the second story was Susan's musical laughter.

"All right, then," Susan told Max, "I'll keep you company...."

"I can't stay," Max said a few minutes later.

"Aw, Maxie," she sighed, "you can't leave. Chicago just wouldn't be the same without you!"

He wondered if Susan would pout that way if she knew it had absolutely no effect on him. She was a nice enough gal; he didn't want to hurt her feelings, but the woman simply couldn't take no for an answer. Even before Melissa died, Susan had put her antennae up, sending signals…hoping Max had received them. He'd picked up on them, all right, but no matter how he tried to tell her he wasn't interested, she hadn't read *his* signals.

"Let me put it another way," he said. "I don't want to stay. Everything and everyone I care about is in Texas."

She pressed close, tilted her head, fluttered her lashes. "Everyone?"

He looked into frosty blue eyes. Pretty eyes, to be sure, but they didn't sparkle with love for him the way Lily's did. "Yeah." He nodded. "Everyone."

Susan lifted her head. "Do you mind if I ask who?"

Max tried to disengage himself from her, but she'd wrapped her arms around him so tightly, he couldn't budge. "Well, my son, for starters. And my mother. She's getting married one of these days—so my step-father, too." He hesitated, wanting to say "Lily" but worried what Susan's reaction might be.

"And Lily?"

Well, there it was, out in the open. So why not admit it? "Yes, Susan. *Especially* Lily."

He thought she looked haughty when her brows went up like that, when she tipped her head and stared at him from the corner of her eye. A little arrogant and a whole lot mean.

"She doesn't have a clue, Max." Susan fiddled with his lapel, tucked the silk handkerchief keeper into his breast pocket. "Don't get me wrong…I'm sure she's *lovely*. But, really, she couldn't be a day over nineteen!"

Leave it to Susan to hit an almost-forgotten sour note. "Lily is twenty-four," he said, hoping he didn't sound as defensive to Susan as he'd sounded to himself.

She laughed softly. "A very young, very naive twenty-four, then."

Without warning, she was stone serious. He'd seen that expression during meetings. The partners rarely left the conference room with a win in their pockets once she'd plastered that look on her pretty face.

Max steeled himself, waiting.

She drew close, even closer than before. "What you need, Maxwell Sheridan," Susan breathed, "isn't a starry-eyed girl, but a woman, a *real* woman who knows how to take care of a man."

He considered reciting the "you'll make some lucky guy a great wife someday" speech, but changed his mind. Because then he'd be forced to tell her *he* was not that man—not now, not ever. Knowing Susan, she'd force him to tell her why. And there simply were no words to explain it—at least, none that wouldn't hurt her.

She combed fingernails through his hair until her hands rested, one on his neck, the other pressed against the back of his head. If a wind had blown through the room right then, Max thought, not a trace of it could have slipped between them. Even if he didn't have a chance with Lily—and would she be here if he didn't?—the situation would have made him uncomfortable. Because his whole life was bottom lines. The bottom line here?

Susan was not his type.

She rested her head on his shoulder, began swaying to and fro, as if to an imaginary waltz. *Enough of this, already!* Max decided. What if someone walked in here and saw them like this?

What if that someone was Lily?

Given the choice between hurting Susan and hurting Lily, well, that wasn't really a choice at all.

He gripped her upper arms, forcing her to take a step back. He hardened his expression and looked into her eyes. "Susan," he said, his voice more stern than it ever had been when scolding Nate, "what do I have to do to make you listen to reason? As soon as I get my house on the market and settle the partnership deal, I'm outta here. Gone. Vamoose. Done with Chicago. For good. Period." He gave her a gentle shake. "Got it?"

Eyes gleaming with challenge, she gave him a half smile. "My, but you're handsome when you're all riled up."

She wrapped a leg around his; if he moved either of his feet, they'd both hit the floor like felled trees.

Max had never backed down from a challenge in his life.

Why start now?

He narrowed his eyes. "So, what's your plan, kid? Keep me standing here 'til Lily comes down those stairs, make sure she gets a good eyeful of you and me like this?"

Susan's eyes filled with tears and she made no attempt to wipe or blink them away. One silvery drop slid down, leaving a white path on her rouged cheek. "You've never even given us a *chance,* Max. How do you know there's nothing here in Chicago for you? *I* could be something. But how will you know if you won't even try?''

She had no way of knowing that Melissa had mastered the art of Crying on Demand. Max had learned to harden his heart to her pseudo-sadness—that, or spend his entire life bending to her every whim, just to keep her quiet.

''I care for you, Max. Very deeply.'' Using one red-polished fingertip, she traced the outline of his upper lip. ''I think you already know that, don't you?'' She looked at him through tear-clumped lashes. ''I think you've always known that.''

''Stop it, Susan,'' he all but growled. ''Stop it right now. You're making a fool of yourself.''

The little-girl-wounded look was gone in a snap. Eyes glittering with anger, she said through clenched teeth, ''No one talks to me that way. *No one.*''

Someone just did, he thought. He gave her a moment to figure that out, then said, ''I'm leaving, so—''

She crooked her leg tighter around his.

Max glared at her. ''You don't honestly think you're gonna change my mind, do you?''

''And you don't think that little girl is gonna make you happy, do you?''

The anger left him, just like that. Max almost thanked her.

''Yeah,'' he said matter-of-factly, ''I do. I love her. More than I've ever loved anyone. And if she'll have me, I want to marry her.''

''Marry her!'' She released his leg, loosened her

hug. "Well, you can't blame a girl for trying, can you?"

Max relaxed. Finally, he'd made her see reason! He made a move to walk away, but she threw herself into his arms and locked her lips to his. Seemed to Max it took a full minute to peel her off him. When at last he succeeded, he didn't look at her, didn't say a word. Instead, he wiped his lips with the back of his hand and stormed from the room.

He'd search every inch of Wilkes's mansion until he found Lily. And when he did, he'd take her in his arms and tell her that he loved her...had from the minute he'd first set eyes on her...would 'til the day he died. Didn't much matter who heard his confession, and he didn't care who saw him get down onto one knee to beg her to be his wife, either.

A few minutes earlier, Lily had been enduring the tour. She had seen some big houses in her day. Her own father's six-thousand-foot rancher boasted six bedrooms, six bathrooms... But this?

The only time she'd seen anything more opulent than Donald Wilkes's home was as a kid, when she and her classmates took a field trip to the state house. That place had four floors, servants' quarters...more rooms than she could count back then. *Give me a simple two-story Victorian any day of the week!* she thought, escaping and half running down the stairs. She hoped that when she found Max, he'd be ready to find the car.

One of the guests, upon learning it was her first visit to Chicago, had said, "You have to visit Navy

Pier while you're here, ride the mile-high Ferris wheel. You can see half the city from up there!''

Going around and around on a hundred-fifty-foot tall ride in Chicago in December sounded like a fun and romantic thing to do. *Great excuse for cuddling!*

She'd had time to think about the whole Max-Susan thing as she traipsed from room to well-appointed room. His roots were in Texas, and so was his heart. She couldn't have been wrong about that. He'd seemed so happy there, so calm and contented. Like all those years ago, when they were just kids and the biggest worry in their lives was whether or not Centennial would win the championships.

He'd been fine-looking then, in his padded red and white uniform. But not nearly as handsome as now.

She had to admit he looked charming in his well-cut suit, looked professional and successful and important, all rolled into one. Lily knew she should have told him so earlier, but she would now...if she could find him again in this labyrinth of rooms and hallways they called a house!

Lily couldn't help remembering the little place across the road from River Valley Ranch. Just a farmette, no more than ten acres. The drive wasn't a twisting, turning black ribbon, like the one her father had built to bring folks from the highway to the house. Instead, it was a straight shot with two narrow lanes of pea gravel that led from the curb to the garage.

It had always been her favorite house. Nowhere in Amarillo had she seen one better. Not too small, but not big enough to get lost in, either. Tall, narrow windows flanked the front door, and Victorian ginger-bread decorated the wraparound porch.

Every day, while waiting for the school bus, she had stared at that house, memorized every board and every brick. Of course she loved the house her father had built, stone upon stone. But *this* house, with its quaint little nooks and crannies, well, it had long been a dream to raise her children in such a house!

Someday, if the Good Lord answered all her prayers, maybe she *would* have a place like that. And maybe the kids who'd leave tricycles and jump ropes on that gorgeous covered porch would be Max's.

Ah, yes…if Lily's memory hadn't failed her, the staircase wound down and down, ending at the library door. And she'd left Max in the—

Lily's heart stopped and her mouth went dry as a bed of cotton. She felt the slick perspiration between her palm and the gleaming oak railing. She tried to move, wanted to move, because the last thing on earth she wanted to do right now was stand here and watch.

Max had both arms wrapped around Susan and was kissing her every bit as earnestly as he had kissed Lily back in Amarillo.

She ran toward the foyer, where a maid had hung her coat and purse. Once she'd stepped outside, where she could think, she'd call for a taxi to take her back to the hotel.

There would be no romantic Ferris-wheel-in-December ride tonight. Or ever.

Chapter Twelve

"Have you seen Lily?" Max asked the senior partner a while later.

"Is she the blonde or the brunette you came in with? I forget." He laughed. "You amaze me, Maxwell. I mean, who else could come in here with bookend beauties!"

If he'd had his way, Max would have walked into the room with only Lily on his arm. Because they'd seen him with women like Susan before, dozens of times. Lily was one of a kind: petite, pretty, with a smile that put the sun's warmth to shame and big green eyes that sparkled brighter than any emerald he'd ever seen. She looked classy in her elegant long-sleeved black dress. Its neckline exposed no more than her collarbones, its hem skimmed the tops of her knees. She'd chosen a single strand of pearls, dangly earrings to match, and piled her hair atop her head so that it looked like a mink-and-satin crown.

"Lily is the brunette."

"Hmm," the man said, nodding. "She's a looker, all right, that one. And she didn't get that way with makeup. No siree. That one was born gorgeous."

Donald stared off into space. Picturing Lily, no doubt, Max thought. A buzz of jealousy coursed through him, and he had a notion to snap his fingers in front of Wilkes's face.

"Um…Lily?" he said instead.

That brought Donald around. "We had quite a pleasant conversation during our little tour. That's some special young woman, your Lily. Pretty as she is on the outside, she's even prettier on the inside."

His Lily. What Max wouldn't give to truly make her his. "Have you seen her?"

Wilkes gave him an "are you kidding?" look. "Last time I saw her, she was headed back to the library. Said that's where she'd left you."

The library, where until a short time ago, he'd been preoccupied with a certain blonde octopus.…

Then Max's heartbeat sped up. Surely he hadn't been *that* preoccupied. He'd have noticed, wouldn't he, if Lily had come into the room while Susan was—

"Mr. Sheridan, sir?"

The partners faced a middle-aged woman in a gray uniform. She smoothed her white apron with one hand, held a gold key ring in the other. "A young woman asked me to give this to you."

Lily had volunteered to stow his car keys in her purse, so he wouldn't have to lug them around all night. How like her to make an offer like that, Max thought, slipping them into his trousers pocket. "Where is the, uh, young lady now?"

"Oh, she left, sir. About half an hour ago."

Now his heart thundered. "Left? But she came with me."

The woman shrugged. "Taxi came for her, like I said, 'bout half an hour ago."

No doubt about it. Lily had seen him with Susan. Why else would she have run off like that?

"Lovers' quarrel?" Donald teased, elbowing Max in the ribs.

"We've never had so much as a cross word," he said, mostly to himself. Then he remembered the time he'd read her the riot act over that whole golden retriever fiasco. "I have to go—see if I can get to the bottom of this."

"Right, before it gets any deeper," Donald agreed. "It's been my experience that diamonds are great smoothing-over tools. My advice to you is, wait until the jewelers open up in the morning before you confront her. If you're going to poke at a hibernating grizzly, be prepared with a tasty treat, I always say."

"Great advice, Don. Thanks for nothing."

Wilkes frowned. "No need to take that tone, Max. Let's not forget who's the senior partner."

"I remember. But I'm outta here, officially, tomorrow. Let's not forget *that*."

Max followed the maid to the door. "Was she very upset when she left?"

"I probably shouldn't say anything, Mr. Sheridan, sir. It's none of my business, after all."

"I'm making it your business."

The woman sighed. "Well, there were tears in her eyes when she walked out that door."

Wincing, Max grabbed his coat from the hall tree and stepped onto the granite porch. He hesitated, remembering he'd driven Susan to the party. He looked back inside. "See that blond woman over there by the piano?"

The maid nodded. "Miss Fisher." She all but scowled. "Yes?"

"I want you to tell her that Max Sheridan said she can hike home or ride on the back of an elephant, for all I care. Don't clean it up—use those words, exactly." He peeled a twenty-dollar bill from his wallet and held it out to her. "I can count on you, right?"

She looked at the money but didn't take it. "Mr. Wilkes doesn't allow us to accept tips from his guests."

"Mr. Wilkes is too pie-eyed to know who's doing what." Max shoved the bill into her apron pocket. "Those words exactly, okay?"

The woman smiled. "It'll be my pleasure, sir."

One more bridge burned, he thought as he started the car.

It was all Max could do to keep his mind on the road during the drive from Wilkes's house to Lily's hotel. He hadn't needed to see her face to imagine how she must have looked, if indeed she'd witnessed the kiss. He cringed, picturing her, green eyes wide with disbelief, lips slightly parted in shock, one delicate hand pressed to her pearl-draped throat. She'd have stood there a second or two, if he knew her, blinking to make sure she hadn't been seeing things. And when she realized the scene was all too real, Lily no doubt had lifted her chin, thrown back her shoulders and marched resolutely toward the nearest exit.

She'd always been a tough little thing. It seemed to Max she'd rather have the earth swallow her whole than allow anyone to see they had enough control over her to make her cry.

He pounded the steering wheel. "Idiot!" he said through his teeth. "What kind of man are you?"

Not the kind she deserved. The guy Lily deserved would have been far more concerned with *her* feelings than with a woman he barely knew. He'd put up with Susan's shenanigans because he hadn't wanted to embarrass her. But it would take a lot more than being brushed off by the likes of him to hurt a woman like that. He'd behaved like the stereotypical ladies' man, believing he was attractive enough, sexy enough to have that kind of power over a woman.

But he *did* have the power to hurt. He'd wounded Lily deeply, cut her to the quick. If he hadn't, she never would have run off like that. Not his take-it-on-the-chin Lily!

He'd never felt more like a heel. When he got right down to it, his own ego had been in control of the situation, not Susan. He hadn't tried hard enough to get rid of her. Who would he be kidding if he said he'd done everything humanly possible?

Certainly not him.

Definitely not Lily.

Max braked hard in her hotel's parking lot and ran from the car to the lobby. He stood, toe tapping nervously on the beige marble floor, waiting for the elevator. When finally it arrived, he got in, punched the button for the fifth floor, drummed his fingers on the brass rail that followed three walls of the car.

The doors opened with a high-pitched *ding* and he stepped into the hall, his hurried footsteps muffled by the plush carpeting. Max found her room, took a deep breath and knocked on the door. He'd make her understand, somehow, that what she'd seen had been a horrible yet meaningless mistake, that nothing like it had ever happened before or would ever happen again.

No answer.

He knocked again, then steeled himself, because if she opened that door and she stood there, eyes red-rimmed from crying...

Still no answer.

Max pressed an ear to the door, knuckles banging a third time. "Lily?" he called quietly. "You in there?"

A bellhop walked by, shoving a cart laden with soiled dishes. "If you're lookin' for the lady who was in that room, I think she checked out."

Max stiffened. "Checked out?"

"Saw her pulling one of those wheely suitcases down the hall." He thought about it a moment. "Must've been ten, fifteen minutes ago, when I delivered room service at the other end of the hall."

"Are you sure she checked out?" He'd floored the sports car, risking a speeding ticket or an accident to get here as fast as he could. How could she have had time to pack and—

"I remember her," the young man said, "because she nearly bumped into me." He tugged the sleeve of his white jacket. "Looked like maybe she'd been cryin'."

"Thanks," Max said, slipping the kid a five.

"Hope you catch up with her," he called, as Max raced toward the bank of elevators.

"So do I," he said under his breath. "So do I...."

Lily decided enough was enough. No more tears. Period. She sat woodenly on the black vinyl chairs at gate nine, hands folded primly in her lap, waiting to board the plane.

She'd been lucky today—catching a standby flight coming into O'Hare, getting another going out.

But luck had nothing to do with it, and she knew it. The Good Lord had orchestrated things.

She learned the hard way, and God had made sure she'd get to Chicago so she could see for herself that things could never work out between her and Max Sheridan. And He'd arranged quick passage home so she could lick her wounds in the bosom of her loving family.

She should have known better. Because, really, what more could she expect from a man who'd abandoned his faith...who, despite his many blessings, questioned the Almighty more often than he questioned local politicians. If he couldn't trust the Lord, how could he be trusted himself?

He can't, she admitted, remembering the sight of him with Susan.

Lily closed her eyes, hoping to block the image from her mind. But it seemed just as vivid, just as painful behind that curtain of darkness.

She focused on the young couple seated across from her. Newlyweds, no doubt. She could tell by the way the girl kept holding her hand up, trying to catch a beam of light in her diamond wedding band. By the way they sat, shoulders touching.

She looked away, unable to watch a moment more of their bliss, because the truth was, she'd never have a moment of it for herself.

True as that was, she couldn't put all the blame on Max's shoulders. Half belonged to her, for convincing herself he cared for her, that maybe he was falling in love with her. He had never said anything of the kind, had never made a single promise, had not so much as hinted at a commitment.

She'd read far more into those kisses than he'd intended. From Max's point of view, they'd probably just been for sport. Trivial. To give meaning to them had been a mistake. One of the biggest she'd made. Ever.

She inhaled a gulp of air, exhaled slowly.

Life was pretty good, right?

She had her dad, her sisters, her animals, right?

Lily remembered a day from long ago...

"Where'd you get that black eye?" her dad had asked, pulling her onto his lap.

"Jimmy Peters dumped my book bag on the school bus floor. And when I was crawling around picking them up, he kicked me. So I socked him. I hate him!" she had said, burying her face in the soft flannel of his plaid shirt.

"Now, now," he said, drying her tears with the pads of his thumbs. "Let me tell you a story. It's about an old Navajo and his young grandson. 'There is a great battle going in within me, a war of two wolves,' he told the boy. 'The first wolf is evil, and symbolizes worry, hatred, bitterness, anger, superiority, laziness—all the worst of human emotions.

"'The second wolf is good, representing kindness and love, hope, faith, trust, helpfulness—the best things man can be.'

"The grandson thought about this for a long, long time, and then he said, 'Grandfather? Which wolf wins?'"

Lamont had taken Lily's face in his big callused hands at that moment, had looked deep into her eyes and finished the story: "'Whichever wolf I feed,' said the grandfather. 'Whichever wolf I feed....'"

Lily hadn't fully understood the moral, not as a ten-year-old.

But she knew its meaning now, and held it close to her heart.

God had blessed her with free will, had given her the ability to choose how she would react to things that happened to her, throughout her life.

She would have to choose now, between feeling disappointed and angry with Max, or forgiving and forgetting. She knew which decision the Lord expected her to make.

So she'd pray, hard, for the strength to get through this quickly, quietly, without complaint.

"Good evening, ladies and gentlemen. Flight number three-five-seven is now boarding at gate nine. If you'll have your boarding pass ready, please..."

Lily stood, grabbed her carry-on bag, and got into

line with her fellow passengers. As she shuffled, one slow step at a time closer to the airliner's entrance ramp, she decided to pray, too, for the wisdom to remember that Max hadn't guaranteed anything but friendship. In that regard, he hadn't let her down at all.

That was the truth she'd hold on to until the pain lessened.

And it would only subside, for it would never leave her.

Max wished he'd left his coat in the car, because as he ran through the terminal, he could feel the sweat running down his back. He checked the monitors, looking for any flight bound for Amarillo International, and saw one, scheduled for takeoff in less than fifteen minutes.

Maybe it would be late and he'd reach her in time, stop her from getting on that plane. He couldn't have her thinking there was any truth in what she'd seen in Wilkes's library.

He tried her cell phone again, hoping she'd finally turned it on. But it rang and rang before a pleasant-voiced woman instructed him to leave a message after the beep. "Lily," he said, breathing hard as he ran toward gate nine, "don't get on that plane. Please. You have to let me explain—"

His cell phone cut out on him. Max slapped the mouthpiece shut. "No-good piece of worthless trash," he grumped, shoving it into his shirt pocket. "Of all the times for it to die on me…"

He encountered a throng of people, milling through

the security check-in point. Max hadn't thought of this. He'd never make it through the system without a boarding pass. Even if he'd managed to book a last-minute flight, he couldn't leave Chicago. Not with all the paperwork he'd put into motion before Wilkes's party. There was no turning back. Not that he wanted to. But if he didn't stay, scribble his John Hancock at the bottom of every document, he'd have to start the whole process over again. No…better to stay put, clean things up, and then put the Windy City behind him, once and for all.

Then he had an idea.

He backtracked a few yards, until he found an available agent at a ticket counter. ''Miss,'' he said, ''I need to have a passenger paged. It's an emergency.''

Seconds later, the woman's voice echoed throughout the terminal: ''Will a Miss Lily London please pick up the nearest airport telephone. Miss Lily London…''

Max waited, pacing back and forth near the security area. There was no other exit from the airport; she'd have to come this way.

The plane was scheduled for takeoff within minutes. Surely she'd already boarded. And, in that case, no way would she have heard the message.

In the unlikely event that she'd arrived moments ago, Lily would be passing through the final leg of security right about now. If she figured out who'd inspired the announcement, would she pick up the phone?

Max rubbed his eyes. No, she wouldn't. And he could hardly blame her.

He walked to the wide wall of windows in time to see an east-west jet taxiing toward the runway. Somehow, Max knew Lily was on that plane.

The best he could hope for now was to redouble his efforts, get the real estate papers signed and get the partnership documents filed. Making a profit was the last thing on his mind.

He took his time heading for the parking lot. No need to hurry now. Just as he stepped into the biting night air, a jetliner screamed overhead, its nose pointed toward the sky. A departing flight, Max thought. Lily's?

"Keep her safe," he whispered sadly into the blackness, "always."

Chapter Thirteen

Lily felt like a silly schoolgirl, avoiding Max's calls this way. Better that, she thought, than to answer the phone and let him hear her bawling on the other end like a starving calf. He'd been tying up loose ends in Chicago for the past few days now. Would he ever tire of leaving messages that never got returned?

She'd learned from Georgia that Max had sold his house in Chicago, that he'd let the partners buy him out of the accounting firm. Which meant that this time, he was coming home for good. According to Georgia he was flying in to Amarillo today.

Lily had to get a handle on her emotions before she talked to him again, because now that he was a full-time Amarillo resident, she'd likely run into him often. When that happened, she wanted to conduct herself with an air of dignity and pride...instead of running off to blubber over unrequited love.

It was as she'd spooned the last of a can of dog food into the one-eyed owl's bowl that the phone rang.

"Lily, Cammi's asking for you. Can you come to the hospital, quick?"

Hospital? Why was Reid at the hospital?

"She lost the baby, kiddo, and she needs you."

Oh, Lord, Lily prayed, *please let it be a mistake!*

"I'm on my way," she told Reid, banging down the phone. "Missy," she told the dog, "you stay here and guard the rest of the guys, okay? I'll be back as soon as I can."

The golden retriever smiled and wagged her tail as if in agreement.

Lily began backing out of the driveway when the biggest pickup truck she'd ever seen pulled in behind her, blocking her in. A tall, lean man got out of the driver's side, strolled up to her car. "You Lily London?"

"Yes," she said tentatively.

"Rangers at Lake Meredith told me you're the gal who's got my dog."

Her heart felt as though it had dropped into her stomach. *No,* she thought, *it can't be. Not after all these months.*

"Come to fetch her," he said, when Lily didn't respond.

She turned off the car, stepped onto the blacktop. "I posted signs, placed ads, even advertised on the radio. But that was months ago."

The man shrugged one bony shoulder. "Been busy."

Lily looked at the truck. A woman sat in the passenger seat, looking every bit as grim-faced and stubborn as the man.

Missy came bounding toward them, stopping several yards away when she spotted the visitor. She wasn't "smiling" now, Lily noticed.

"She never did cotton to me," he said, rolling a toothpick from one side of his mouth to the other. With his thumb, he gestured toward the truck. "Belongs to my wife."

"I've grown very fond of Missy...."

At the sound of her name, the retriever's ears perked. Still, she remained a safe distance from the man.

"Missy? Her name ain't Missy. It's Yella Gold— Goldie for short." He inspected grimy fingernails. "Tell you what," he said, chomping on the toothpick, "since you're so smitten with the mutt, I'll sell her to you."

Lily had her checkbook, right there on the front seat of her car. She reached over the console to grab it. "Name your price," she said, opening it up and clicking the ballpoint she kept inside its case.

"Ten thousand dollars."

Her mouth dropped open. "Ten thousand..." She looked at Missy and knew that if she had that kind of money, she'd gladly pay it. But Lily poured every penny of what she earned managing River Valley Ranch into the care and feeding of her animals. "I...I don't have that much." She glanced at the register, saw the dismal total on the bottom line.

She narrowed her eyes, suddenly suspicious. "How do I know she's your dog?"

He smirked, pulled a sheet of folded paper from his shirt pocket. ''Kinda thought you might ask that,'' he said, handing it to her. ''That's her pedigree you're holdin'.''

She glanced at it, tried to hand it back. ''This is still no proof that you're her owner.''

He wouldn't accept the paper. ''So, it's proof you want, is it?'' The man faced Missy and snapped his fingers. Her fur bristled as she bared her teeth. A low, ferocious growl echoed from deep in her chest as she lowered her head. ''Goldie,'' he ordered, ''come!''

Missy's snarling intensified. She hadn't shown any signs of being vicious, not once in the months since Lily had pulled her out of Lake Meredith. ''Where'd you lose her?'' she demanded.

''Me an' the missus was fishin' on Lake Meredith. She fell in the water.'' He shrugged again. ''We thought she drowned. Then I found this.''

The paper he handed her this time was one of the Lost Dog posters she'd hung on every telephone pole in Amarillo. ''I still haven't seen any proof that you're her owners.''

''Kinda thought you'd say that, too,'' he said, ''bein' that you're Lamont London's baby girl and all. Here's the check I wrote to the kennel, and the one I wrote to the American Kennel Club. See? The numbers jibe. She's my dog.''

Now Lily understood. They'd heard that her father was one of the wealthiest men in the Texas Panhandle; they'd put two and two together, and come up with ten thousand.

Well, she couldn't ask her dad for the money. Lamont had always been generous to a fault. But he'd been born and raised a rancher, with a practical, down-to-earth mind-set about money. To him, animals were a family's bread and butter. No dog, not even his beloved Obnoxious, would be worth ten thousand dollars.

"I can give you five hundred now, five hundred more if—"

"Nope. Ten grand. Take it or leave it."

It made sense, suddenly, that they'd named her Goldie. Who knows how many times they'd pulled this scam?

Maybe if she could buy some time… "Could you give me a few days?"

He glanced at his wife, who gave one slow nod.

"You have a week." He checked his watch, then climbed into the driver's seat of his truck. "Ten grand," he repeated, "or the mutt goes home with us."

With that, he backed down the drive and headed north.

Trembling, heart hammering, Lily hugged Missy. "Those terrible people!" she said, kissing the dog's head. "What have they done to you?" Ruffling the retriever's long, shiny ears, she added, "Don't you worry, girl. I'll find a way to keep you." She kissed her again, this time on her snout.

Lily got back into the car and headed south, toward the hospital. "When it rains, it pours," she muttered. With Cammi in the hospital and Missy's future in jeopardy, she'd have plenty to worry about.…

Her father's wolf story came to mind.

Which wolf are you going to feed? she asked herself.

Cammi had always been Lily's rock. Since they lost their mother when Lily was four and Cammi twelve, her sister had been more like a mom. Now it was Lily's turn to be the supportive, nurturing one.

Cammi would need her to be strong. So would Reid, for that matter. Could she do it?

She could…if she fed the right wolf.

Home. Max had thought about it as he signed the real estate papers, as he scribbled the bottom line on the documents that would free him from the partnership, as he read the in-flight magazine during the trip home.

It sure would be good to unpack in Amarillo, never to live anywhere else again.

But there were more important things to consider than his suitcase. He had to straighten things out with Lily—the sooner, the better.

He must have called her fifty times since she left Chicago the other night, must have left half that many messages. But she hadn't answered one. Maybe he'd been wrong on Thanksgiving when he'd speculated which of Lamont's daughters had inherited his fiery temper. Maybe it *was* Lily, not Violet, after all. Because if she wasn't mad at him, what kept her from answering the phone!

Hurt feelings, that's what. In her shoes, he'd have been humiliated, witnessing what looked like a passionate love scene. But unlike Lily, Max would have confronted things, head-on.

Wouldn't he?

He'd driven straight from the airport to River Valley Ranch, fully expecting to find Lily in the barn, mothering her animals.

He'd been wrong.

Missy had been there and, strange as it seemed, hadn't acted like her usual happy self. "What's wrong, girl?" he asked, ruffling her soft fur. "You missin' your mama?"

The dog whined, broke free of his hug and began pacing. Something had agitated her, and Max couldn't help but wonder what. Missy was the most laid-back dog he'd ever met.

He knocked on the back door of Lamont's ranch house.

No answer.

He tried the front door.

Same result.

That was almost as weird as Missy's behavior, because not once in all the years he'd come here as a boy had the place been deserted.

It was like a ghost town. No Lamont. No Lily. Not even a ranch hand he could quiz.

Puzzled and worried, Max left.

"I don't get it," Max said, a short while later in Georgia's diner. "What do you mean, someone wants ten grand for Missy?"

Georgia shrugged. "I'm only repeating what I heard in town. Strangers showed up, put papers under Lily's nose to prove they're the dog's rightful owners. She has a week to come up with the money or Missy goes with them next time they leave." She pointed to the bulletin board near the phone. "That's their number."

"How'd *you* get it?"

"They came here first, looking for her, while she was out visiting you in Chicago. Told me if I heard from her, I should have her call them." She paused. "How'd things go out there, anyway?"

"Don't ask."

"Max Sheridan, you can't say a thing like that to a woman and get away with it!"

He knew it was true. Particularly with *this* woman. Max told her all about it—about how surprised he'd been when she called to say she'd taken him up on his invitation, about the dinner party…about Susan.

"Good grief, Max. What were you thinking!"

"That's just the trouble. I wasn't."

"Well, what're you going to do?"

He shrugged. "Mom, I honestly don't know."

"You love her, don't you?"

"Big time," he said without hesitation.

"Then, you have to set her straight, as soon as possible."

"She'll probably never speak to me again."

"'Course she will. She loves you, too."

"Wish I could be sure of that."

"Trust me. I've been people-watching my whole adult life. This place gives me plenty of opportunity to hone up on it. I know the difference between infatuation and 'til-death-do-you-part love. That girl's got a bad case of the 'I Love Max' blues."

He met her eyes. "Y'think?" he asked hopefully.

"I *know*." She took a sip of coffee. "Trouble is, she's as stubborn as that bear of a father of hers. If she's got it in her head to stay away from you, that's exactly what she'll do."

He frowned. "Man. I hope not."

"I remember years back, when you were off at college, she was working for me part time. One of the young truckers who came in a couple of times a week did something to rile her. She'd walk *way* around his table here in the diner." Using her chin as a pointer, she indicated the street. "Out there, she'd go clean across the street to avoid him."

"Whew. What did he do to get her that mad?"

"Never did find out. But I can promise you this— if that fella walked in here right now, and Lily saw him, she'd head straight out the door."

Talk like this wasn't helping build his confidence any. Max said, "So, is she going to give the money to Missy's owners?"

"Don't see how she can. She puts every dime she gets her hands on into those animals of hers."

"What about Lamont? Surely he'd help her."

She gave him a hard stare. "You're joking, right?"

Max sighed. "I guess that is pretty ridiculous." He'd lived in cattle country most of his life. Dogs were for protection, for herding cows. Sure, folks got attached to them, but not ten thousand dollars' worth of attachment. It just wasn't practical. "She must be brokenhearted," he said. "She loves that dog almost as much as I love Nate."

"Shame it had to happen right now, too. She's already got enough on her shoulders, considering what's going on with Cammi and Reid.''

''What's going on?''

Georgia sighed. ''That poor girl…she came back to town a year or so ago. Did you hear she'd gone to Hollywood, tried to become an actress?''

''Doesn't surprise me. Cammi always did love the stage. And she's the spitting image of her mom.''

''Rose could have been a big star if she hadn't married Lamont. She'd gotten top billing in a dozen or so movies before they met.''

''Think she regretted giving it up?''

''Not a chance. She was born to be by his side.''

Max understood that only too well. He'd loved Lily for just about as long as he could remember.

''Cammi got married out there, some stuntman.''

''I hadn't heard that.''

''It's true. The young fool took risks all day long on the movie sets, and would you believe he died when he crashed his car into a tree?''

Max shook his head as he poured himself a cup of coffee.

''Poor kid tried her best out there, but she couldn't make ends meet. Told me that on the very afternoon she buried her husband, the doctor called to tell her she was gonna have a baby.''

''But…''

''She lost that one, too.''

''What do you mean, 'too'?''

''What do you think it means?''

Max winced. ''Man. That's rough.''

Nodding, Georgia sighed again. ''The whole family

is at the hospital, lending moral support. I imagine it's hardest for Lily, because she and Cammi have always been closer than sisters.''

He should go over there, lend moral support to *her*. But what if his presence only upset her more?

''If you had the sense God gave a goose, you'd go over there, hold her hand.''

''She'd probably slug me.''

''So, let her. You've got it coming.''

''Hey. Whose side are you on?''

''I'll tell you whose. If this cane reached farther, I'd smack you upside your head. What were you thinking, letting that hussy—''

''I already told you. I wasn't thinking.''

Not clearly, anyway. But he was thinking rationally now. He downed the coffee in one gulp, then headed for the door, stopping near the corkboard. He snapped the slip of paper bearing the name and number of Missy's owners from under its peg, shoved it into his shirt pocket.

Georgia smiled. ''Careful, son.''

''Why?''

''People are gonna get the idea you have a heart, after all.''

Truth was, he didn't care what people thought. Aside from his mother and son, the only opinion of him that really mattered was Lily's.

And he intended to do everything in his power to prove it to her, starting now.

When he'd left River Valley before his trip to Chicago, Max had seen Hank's sister at the house across the road, carrying a For Sale sign to the front porch. He'd heard that Gladys and George were thinking of moving to Florida; evidently, they'd made their decision.

Now Max had more than enough time to check things out. Nate was playing happily with Georgia's old baking pans when he left his mom's apartment. Georgia's plan, she'd told Max, was to "teach that boy to make his *own* chocolate-chip cookies, since he eats them by the dozen!" As he pulled into the driveway, he remembered that when others commented on Lamont London's regal ranch house, Lily always shrugged. "I'd rather live in a house like the Morgans'," she'd say. "It's my dream house." If he'd heard that once, he'd heard it a hundred times.

He fully intended to keep the diner, but Max didn't want to live in the apartment upstairs anymore. He yearned for a lush green lawn, a yard for Nate to play in, a vegetable garden, a garage where he could putter with his woodworking tools. If he bought the Morgan place...

He'd gone to high school with Pat; maybe she could help him cut through some red tape.

"It needs some work," she admitted, showing him around inside. "But it's a good, solid house. I'd bet it'll still be standing here when both of us are six feet under."

"Now, there's a cheery thought," he teased. He walked outside, grabbed the For Sale sign. He handed it to her. "I want it."

Laughing, she said, "You don't even know the asking price."

"Doesn't matter. I'll take it." He handed her a business card, scratched out his Chicago information and scribbled in his new numbers. "Call me when you've drawn up the paperwork."

"Max, don't you want an inspector's report?"

"Yeah, but whatever is wrong can be fixed. You said yourself it's a good solid house."

"Well…"

"How long will it take?"

"Couple of hours, if the Morgans take your offer."

"Make them an offer they can't refuse. Top their asking price by five grand."

"Max!" Pat said, fanning herself with his business card. "You're supposed to talk them *down,* not jack the price *up!*"

He glanced at the wrought-iron archway across the road. If Lily said no the first time he proposed, he'd be nice and close; it would be real easy to show up unannounced and pop the question again and again 'til he wore down her resistance and she said yes, if only to shut him up.

"I want it," he said again. "I'll pay cash."

She opened her mouth to protest, but he held up a hand to stop her. "Have the papers ready by morning and I'll double your percentage."

Pat didn't need to think about it. "Done!" she said, grinning.

Now, as he pulled into a space in the hospital parking lot, he smiled to himself. He wasn't going to let Lily get away this time. He'd waited twelve years to make her his own. If it took another twelve before she said "I do," so be it. And in the meantime, he wouldn't have to wake up to the smell of frying bacon every morning of his life!

He stopped at the desk, asked where he might find Reid and Cammi and the rest of the Londons. Third floor, Maternity Ward, the lady in the striped smock told him. That seemed cruel, Max thought, putting a woman who'd just lost her baby among new mothers and newborns....

On his way to the elevator, he spied the gift shop. Inside, he bought two bouquets of flowers: pink roses for Cammi, red ones for Lily. He bought chocolates, too, and a card that said "My thoughts are with you." He signed it while the cashier rang up his order, tucked it into Cammi's blooms. "If you need any-thing," he wrote, "just say the word." Max drew a line under *anything,* and signed his name.

What does a man say in a situation like this? he wondered as the elevator took him up two floors. "I'm sorry," while sincere, seemed weak and inad-equate. Might be best to say nothing, shake Reid's hand, hand Cammi the roses—tell them how he felt, just by being there. Maybe something profoundly genuine would strike him once he was in their pres-ence.

Lamont and Nadine, Violet and Ivy had gathered in the waiting room. Max studied their joyless faces and waited for something wise and comforting to come to mind. When it didn't, he sat in the nearest empty chair. "Sorry to hear what happened. Is Cammi okay?"

"Physically, she's fine," Nadine said.

No one needed to spell out how she was doing emotionally.

"Nice of you to come," Vi said. "Are the flowers for Cammi?"

He nodded, shoved the vase of pink roses closer to her. "You can take them to her. I don't want to intrude."

"We appreciate your being here, son," Lamont said.

His deep voice was foggy with grief, something Max understood only too well. Watching a child of your blood suffer was hard and painful, especially if there wasn't a blessed thing you could do about it. Parents were supposed to protect their kids from harm, dads in particular....

"Lily is in the chapel," Ivy said. She smiled sadly. "I take it the other bunch is for her?"

Max nodded.

"Well, go on," Lamont instructed. "Take 'em to her before they wilt. And don't forget the chocolates. Lily has loved the stuff since before she cut her first tooth."

He got to his feet, hesitated.

"Chapel is one floor up, end of the hall," Ivy told him.

"Thanks," he said, and headed for the elevator.

"Lord," he whispered, "get me through this."

He couldn't believe his own ears. Had a *prayer* really just come out of his mouth? No wonder, he thought as the elevator doors closed, with all the tragedy and trauma that had been going on lately.

What would he say when he found Lily?

Would words even be necessary?

He'd get down on his hands and knees if that's what it took, because he wanted her to be a permanent part of his life—the sooner the better.

When he peered through the arched window carved into the door, the chapel appeared to be empty. But then he saw her, seated in front, her head bowed.

Easing the door open, Max stepped inside, the bloodred carpet dulling his footfalls. He walked up the center aisle and stopped beside her. *Hi, Lil,* he wanted to say. Instead, he tucked the box of candy under his arm and laid a hand on her shoulder.

She didn't move, save for the slightest intake of air. For a moment Lily merely sat, staring straight ahead. Then she placed her warm hand atop his, gave it a gentle *pat, pat, pat,* and slid over in the pew to make room for him.

"Peace offering?" she whispered, pointing to the candy on his lap, the roses in his hand.

He tucked in one side of his mouth. She had a knack for reading his mind, and he said so.

"What you saw in Chicago," he started.

She held up a hand to silence him.

"It wasn't what you think," he continued.

Lily met his eyes and he read the hopeful expectation there.

"I was explaining to Susan that…" He coughed. "I was…"

"…telling her goodbye?" she finished for him.

Max smiled. "That, and then some."

He watched her left brow rise slightly, as if the unasked question was too much to bear. This wasn't the time or the place for romantic admissions. He'd tell her the "and then some" when the time *was* right. He gently changed the subject.

"I'm sorry, Lily, about Cammi's baby, about…" He blew a stream of air through his lips. "About a lot of things."

Lily opened the box of candy, popped a vanilla cream into her mouth. "So am I," she said around it.

"You?" He turned slightly in the seat, draping an arm along the pew back behind her. "What could you possibly have to be sorry for!"

"Just…things." She held out the box, offered him a piece. When he shook his head, she bit into a solid chocolate.

"What things?"

She met his eyes. "Does it matter?"

He could see that she'd been crying, that she was struggling to staunch tears, even now. Max wanted to wrap her in his arms, protect her from pain of any kind. Instead, he grazed his knuckles across her satiny cheek.

"No," he whispered. "It doesn't matter."

She tilted her head, hugging his fingertips to her shoulder. Such a sweet gesture. So sweet that he shifted, intending to hold her close, to start the litany of excuses for his awful behavior.

But she lifted the flowers to her face, closed her eyes and inhaled. "Amazing, aren't they?"

"Amazing?" Max sat back. *All in good time,* he thought. "How so?"

"Well, they're so delicate. Soft as velvet. You could crush one with your bare hands. And yet…"

She sighed, drew in their perfume again. "And yet they're tough enough to slice through denim. I know, because it's happened to my blue jeans when I hiked in the—" She looked up at him again. "I'm boring you."

"You couldn't bore me, not even if you tried. Now go on. You were hiking…"

"The point is, nothing is what it seems."

When she looked at him this time, he read the challenge in her eyes. So many things she could be referring to… But Max didn't dare ask what, for fear he'd mention the wrong one, give her a whole new reason to avoid him.

"Get your cell phone fixed?" he asked, changing the subject.

Lily blinked. "It isn't broken." Then a slow smile broadened her mouth as she realized what he was getting at. "I've been…busy."

"So I take it." He stroked her cheek again. "I'm sorry about Cammi's baby."

Lily nodded. "Me, too."

He took his arm from the pew, rested it across her shoulders. "Is there anything I can do?"

When she smiled up at him, his heart lurched.

"You're already doing it, Max."

"How's she doing?"

"Pretty good, all things considered. They'll be sending her home in the morning. Nothing more the doctor can really do."

"I guess she's taking it pretty hard?"

"No harder than would be expected. But she's been through it before. She'll be okay, in time."

Max faced forward, pressed the pads of his fingertips together to form a spider that squatted and stood, squatted and stood. "Doesn't seem fair."

"What doesn't?"

"With a world of wicked, evil people to pick on, why did God choose Cammi to do this to? She's as good as gold."

"He isn't picking on her," Lily corrected. "It just…" She shrugged again. "It just happened. It isn't God's fault."

"Then, whose fault is it?"

"I guess if we need to name a culprit, we can choose life."

He shook his head. "I'll never understand you people."

"'You people'?"

"Believers. Followers. Born-again, saved, baptized, in-the-spirit Christians—whatever you're calling yourselves these days."

She pursed her lips, tilted her head. "I like to think we're the faithful."

"See, that's where you lose me."

"Where faith comes in, you mean?"

He nodded.

"You can't have faith by taking a pill, Max. It doesn't magically show up in some people, skip over others. It's something that develops, over time. Something that you learn to *do* as much as you learn to *feel.*…"

"Through suffering?"

"Not necessarily, but that's one road."

"Thanks, but I think that's one road I'll stay off of. Too many potholes."

"You put them there. You should be able to avoid them."

He turned to her. "What?"

"Well, you did." She replaced the top on the candy box. "Every time you feel doubt, or fear, or worry, you're digging a new hole. See, that's where I was going before, with all that 'rose' talk. We're a lot like those flowers. We sometimes look weak and fragile, but we're really not.

"Because God made us of strong stuff, gave us what we need to fend off things like doubt and fear and worry. You have all the tools you need to avoid those potholes—right here." She laid her hand over his heart. "*That's* where faith is born, Max. You can't get it simply by showing up at church, or by reading the Bible. You won't find it by donating money to charity or doing good deeds."

She patted his chest. "You'll find it *here,* within yourself." A last shrug. "If you choose not to look, then you have no one to blame but yourself when your tires go flat."

"Tires?"

"Well, the potholes metaphor was yours...."

He chuckled. Leave it to her to make him laugh, even at a time like this. Max put his arm around her again. "So you're really okay with what happened to Cammi's baby?"

"I didn't say that. I'm heartbroken. I'm sad. Angry. It shouldn't have happened. She'd make a wonderful mother." She took his hands in hers, gave them a gentle shake. "Don't you get it? I have faith that things will turn out all right in the end. I have no idea *how* they'll turn out, mind you, but I know everything will be all right."

"And that's faith."

"My version of it, anyway."

He pulled her into a sideways hug. "How'd you get so smart?" he asked, kissing her temple.

"Not smart..."

"Faithful," they said together.

"I'm not sure I get it," he admitted, "but I promise you this—I'm going to give what you said a lot of thought."

"Why the sudden change of heart?"

He could almost feel the warmth of her little hand against his chest, above his heart. "Truth?"

Eyes wide, she pointed to the cross up front. "You're in a church," she said, grinning. "I strongly advise it."

He'd been beating himself up over Melissa's death for far too long. Logic and common sense told him it wasn't his fault that the poor girl had overdosed. Still...

But Lily had a point. Maybe. If she was right about this whole faith thing, maybe he could let go of the past.

No maybes about it, Max thought; if Lily was at his side, he could overcome *anything*.

"I don't want to lose you again, Lily. If learning how to have faith will keep you in my life, it's as good as done."

''We go too far back for you to worry about anything like that.''

She'd misunderstood, thought he meant he didn't want to lose her *friendship*. Sure, he wanted that, because what kind of marriage would it be without it? But he wanted more. All of it. The whole ball of wax. Fireworks, hearts and flowers, bells and whistles, the whole nine romantic yards.

Max grabbed her shoulders, forced her to meet his eyes, gave her a gentle shake. He wanted to say, *I love you and I want to spend the rest of my life with you!* But that look in her eyes—that spark of suspicion, that glint of mistrust—choked off the words.

He pressed a tender kiss to her forehead, then gathered her near. ''Ah, Lily,'' he sighed into her hair. Soon, he'd tell her everything she needed to hear— and a few things she hadn't even considered yet.

But not here, not now. He had a lot of work to do first, to earn her trust, to smother her suspicion.

''Want to go back to Cammi's room?''

She nodded.

He gathered up the flowers and the chocolate, then slid an arm around her and led her into the hall.

Yes, he had a lot of work to do. But he had time. And when he had finished, things would be all right.

Funny, but suddenly he believed that. *Really* believed it.

Smiling, Max understood why.

He'd found the meaning of faith.

Chapter Fourteen

After the Christmas Eve service, parishioners gathered on the church steps, laughing and talking, sharing holiday plans. Max hadn't felt this welcomed or at ease, anywhere, in a long time.

"Your mom did *what?*"

"Eloped. Left a note and everything."

Lamont chuckled. "No foolin'?"

Max pretended to read it: "'Dear Son, Running off to get married. Take care of my cane.'"

Laughing, Lamont said, "Well, she spared you the fuss and bother of a wedding. Count your blessings."

He found himself doing that a lot lately, thanks to Lily.

A week or so before Christmas, she'd introduced him to the writings of Henry Van Dyke. Max hadn't expected to like the poems and essays, but read them because he had promised Lily he would. No one was more surprised than Max when the simple yet beautiful words reminded him of God's awesome power.

As a result, he'd gone back to church—not because Georgia needed a ride or Nate wanted to attend a social, but because his rediscovered sense of peace had drawn him into the fellowship.

"Speaking of marriage," Max said, taking Lamont aside, "there's something I'd like to talk to you about."

Backs to the rest of the crowd, the men stood just around the corner of the church.

"I'm sure you know how I feel about Lily...."

Lamont smiled. "I've known since you were both still in school."

Nodding, Max said, "I figured as much. So I was wondering...what would you say if I asked her to marry me?"

As the awkward moment of silence ticked by, Max realized he hadn't considered what he'd do if Lamont didn't give his consent. He wouldn't go against the man's wishes.

Or would he?

He loved Lily, more than he'd ever imagined it was possible to love another human being. But without her father's blessing, life might prove to be difficult at best.

Lamont gave Max a fatherly slap on the back. "I'd say it's about time, that's what!"

Overwhelmed with gratitude and relief, Max threw his arms around his father-in-law to be. "Thanks, Lamont." He stepped back, ran both hands through his hair. "I'll be good to her. You've got my word on it."

He looked at the older, wiser face, read the mischievous expression and prepared for a "you will if you know what's good for you" speech.

"I don't doubt it for a minute," Lamont said instead. Abruptly, he turned, guided Max back toward the church entrance. "Tell you what," he said. "There's no sense in your going home, spending Christmas Eve alone. You're coming to dinner anyway, so why don't you and Nate stay in the guest room tonight." He paused, then added, "I think it would do us all a lot of good, having a child in the house on Christmas morning."

Cammi and Reid hadn't been out of the house until tonight's service. He'd half expected they'd be sullen and withdrawn, burdened by their grief. They'd been anything but! The newlyweds looked genuinely happy. Surely there would still be private moments of mourning, but it was clear that their faith had pulled them through.

"Thanks, Lamont," Max said. "Nate would love that...and so would I."

Lily's dad grinned. "Once there's a ring on her finger, feel free to call me 'Dad.'"

He'd noticed that's how Reid referred to the man; Max was touched to be so easily included into the London family. "Thanks," he said again, meaning it.

One more blessing to be counted....

"This is really nice of you," Max said at the London house later that evening. "If I wrapped them, Nate's presents would look like a gorilla had done it."

Lily pointed to the one gift Max *had* wrapped and

grinned. "I see what you mean." Then she added, "Don't think I'm doing it for nothing."

He took a step closer. "So there's a price tag on the gesture?"

"Mmm-hmm," she said around a length of curly ribbon, "big one. You have to help me decorate the cookies."

"You're joking. Knowing what a klutz I am, you'd—"

"The cookies need to look festive, not store-bought. Your touch is exactly what the job calls for."

"Okay, if you say so...."

"This is my favorite night of the year."

"Why's that?"

"Well, listen to the house, all hushed and peaceful. I wonder if it sounded like this in the manger, the night Christ was born?"

Max took her in his arms. "Not likely, with all those cows and donkeys. And let's not forget that kid with his drum."

Lily laughed. "And you call *me* silly!"

He glanced at the tree. "Your dad tells me you decorated the tree all by yourself."

She nodded.

"Decorated the whole house."

Another nod. "And your point is?"

"Answer me something…"

"Yes?"

"How'd you get the angel up there? That tree must be twenty feet tall."

"Fifteen. But only because we're limited by the ceiling. And to answer your question, I got the angel up there with the aid of a handy little invention known as the stepladder. Amazing contraption. Every house oughta have one.''

''Nut,'' he said. He drew her closer. ''What if this was your standard eight-foot ceiling?''

''Then, I guess we'd have a seven-foot tree.'' Grinning as her brow furrowed, Lily said, ''Why do you ask?''

A smug little grin turned up one corner of his mouth. ''Oh, nothing. Just wondering, that's all.'' Max glanced around the room. ''Where's Missy?''

''Upstairs in the guest room…on the foot of Nate's bed.''

Max chuckled. ''I should have known. That kid loves her.''

''She loves him, too.''

Another all-knowing little grin. Then he said, ''Yeah, she does.''

Lily grabbed his wrist, started rolling up his shirt-sleeve.

''What're you doing?''

''Just checking to see what's up there.'' She gave him a wary glance. ''You've been acting like the cat that swallowed the canary all evening. What's up?''

He let go of her, headed for the tree. Down on one knee, he wiggled his eyebrows. ''What-say we open one present tonight?''

''Max! We can't do that! It's—''

''It's past midnight. Technically, it's Christmas morning. C'mon. What do you say?''

He looked so much like an innocent boy at that moment, with the colorful lights reflecting in his big

dark eyes, that Lily didn't know how she could refuse. "All right," she said, joining him on the floor,
"but just one."

"One'll do it," he said, grabbing the package he'd
wrapped.

Lily slid one of his presents from a small stack; if
he opened this one tonight, he'd be able to wear it
tomorrow.

He took her hand, led her to the couch. "You
first," he said, patting the cushion beside him.

"No...*you* first."

"But what about the old rule—Ladies First?"

"I like to shake things up once in a while. Gentleman can be at the front of the line...sometimes." She
nodded toward his gift. "Go ahead. Open it."

She'd spent half an hour getting the foil paper
tucked over the corners—just right; arranging the
wide bow—just so. Max tore into it in less than a
second, it seemed. Laughing as he lifted the lid, she
said, "What took you so long!"

He dug through the tissue paper and pulled out the
sweater. "It's great," he said. "I hope it's big
enough." He looked inside the collar. "Hey, there's
no label."

"That's because I made it."

Max stared at her, blinking as the information sunk
in.

"A homemade sweater?" He held it up to his
chest. "You *made* this?"

She nodded.

"When did you have time?"

"I had hours and hours, in the barn. If one of the

animals is bad-off, I spend the night out there, to keep an eye on things. Can't risk dozing off, so I do stuff like that to keep myself awake.''

"You spent hours and hours on *me?*"

Smiling, she said, "You're worth it."

Max studied the intricate cabling that decorated the sweater's front. "It's beautiful." He met her eyes. "I'm impressed."

"Don't be," she said. "I'm not."

"That's exactly what I said to you in Chicago, when you saw my office."

He was right, and it touched her that he remembered something so seemingly trivial. Maybe he'd been telling the truth that day in the hospital chapel, when he'd said he had much to prove to her.

"Your turn," he said, pointing to the box on her lap.

Lily deliberately took her time peeling off the stick-on bow, picking at the cellophane tape that held the Christmas-stockings paper in place. The waiting was driving him crazy, and she knew it. Smiling, she slowed her pace even more.

"You have exactly ten seconds," he said, his voice quiet and deep, "to open that box. After that, *I'm* gonna do it for you." He pulled back his shirtsleeve to expose his watch, and started counting. "Ten, nine, eight…"

"All right, spoilsport, have it your way." Lily lifted off the lid and pulled back the crinkled white tissue paper. "It's…it's a…" She met his eyes. "A dog leash?"

"Uh-huh. But there's more. Keep digging."

She found an envelope buried in the bottom and slid out its contents. Missy's pedigree! "Max," she sighed, heart thumping with relief and joy and love. "How did you... When did you? I can't believe it!" She threw her arms around him, kissed him soundly on the cheek. "So she's mine? For real?"

"That's what the papers say."

"Maxwell Sheridan, I love you!"

"Yeah, yeah," he said, pushing her away. "Quit stalling. There's more in that envelope."

Lily couldn't help but notice...he hadn't said he loved her, too.

Sighing, she focused on his instructions. When she shook the envelope, a key fell into her upturned palm. The key to his heart? *Fat chance,* Lily thought.

"What does it open?"

"A door."

"A door," she echoed. "*What* door?"

"To a house."

"A house," she said, her voice a dull monotone as the frustration built. "*What* house?"

"The one across the road."

She looked toward the front door. "The Morgan place?" Frowning, Lily said, "Max, what on earth are you doing with their house key!"

"Isn't theirs," he said calmly. And poking a finger into her chest, he added, "It's yours."

"Mine? But..." She didn't understand.

"Okay. All right." He leaned forward, balancing elbows on knees, and clasped his hands in the space between. "Maybe this will clear things up...." He held her left hand in his and looked deep into her eyes. "What would you say if I told you Missy and the house across the road are yours to keep?"

"I'd say, 'Will you marry me?'" she blurted. Instantly, her fingertips went to her lips. Too late—the words were already out. In the space of two minutes, she'd succeeded in saying *everything* guaranteed to scare a confirmed bachelor into the next county.

He huffed. "You're not even gonna get down on one knee?"

Lily blinked. "I'm not— *What?*"

"And here I thought you were an old-fashioned girl, one who treasured tradition. Boy—" he shook his head "—was I wrong."

"Max, I—"

"When you ask a guy to marry you, you're supposed to get down on one knee. Take his hand in yours. Look longingly into his eyes. *Then* you say, 'Will you do me the honor of becoming my husband'?"

Lily's breathing was coming in short, soft gasps, her heart pounding like a parade drum. "And if I did all that," she began, not even caring that her voice trembled, that her hands quaked, "what would you say?"

He answered by taking her face in his hands. "I'd say, 'I love you, with all my heart. Always have, always will. And I could kick myself for not realizing it years ago, so we could be married by now!'" He paused, smiled. "*Then* I'd say, 'What took you so long to ask!'" He kissed the tip of her nose.

"So…is that a yes?"

"Say yes, Dad!" Nate said, jumping up and down in the doorway. "Say yes!"

Missy joined the three-way hug, tail wagging and doggy lips grinning.

"Well," Nate said, frowning at his father. "What are you waiting for?" He smacked the heel of his hand to his forehead.

"Say it!"

"Yes," he breathed.

"Hooray!" Nate hollered.

"Shh," Lily rustled his dark curls. "You'll wake everyone up."

"Sorry...Mom."

Tears sprang to her eyes as she looked into the merry little face.

"Get a load o' *that*," Max said. "One minute you're footloose and fancy free, the next..."

The answers to every prayer she'd prayed for herself were right here in this room. Lily had a feeling this would be the most memorable Christmas ever.

"Mom," she whispered. "Accidentally, sort of, but, *Mom!*"

Dear Reader,

Some of my all-time favorite poems and stories were composed by Henry van Dyke (1852–1933). The words of this gentle Pennsylvania-born man, who spent his life pastoring in New York and teaching English literature at Princeton, have been touching readers' hearts since his first works were published.

I wish Max Sheridan, my hero in *An Accidental Mom*, had discovered van Dyke's writings earlier; maybe then he wouldn't have slipped so far from his Father's guiding hand....

For the poet's guileless words remind us how simple it is to invite God into our lives, how very eager He is to accept our invitation. Perhaps a word, a phrase from the quiet, thought-provoking verses would have spared Max years of cold, lonely searching.

If you, like Max, find yourself a little lost, a little too far from the restful solace of the Almighty's embrace, do yourself a favor and read as many of Henry van Dyke's poems and stories as you can get your hands on. I promise, you won't regret it!

If you enjoyed *An Accidental Mom*, drop me a note c/o Steeple Hill Books, 233 Broadway, Suite 1001, New York, NY 10279. I love hearing from my readers, and try to answer every letter personally.

All my best,

Loree Lough

P.S. Watch for my next book in the ACCIDENTAL BLESSINGS series, *Accidental Family*, because in this one, Lily and Cammi's dad, Lamont London, is the hero!

Love Inspired

A HERO FOR DRY CREEK

BY

JANET TRONSTAD

Every night, rancher and secret romantic
Nicki Redfern asked God for a handsome prince
with strong faith to sweep her away. And then
tuxedo-clad Garrett Hamilton showed up on her
doorstep, with a limousine and her long-lost
mother. Was Garrett the answer to her prayers?

Don't miss

A HERO FOR DRY CREEK
On sale November 2003

Available at your favorite retail outlet.

SEPTEMBER LOVE

BY

VIRGINIA MYERS

Fiftysomething Beth Colby thought her life was complete—after years of being a single mother and widow, she found a second chance at love, with Doug Colby. But was her new marriage ready for the permanent addition of Doug's rambunctious toddler grandson?

Don't miss

SEPTEMBER LOVE

On sale November 2003

Available at your favorite retail outlet.

ONCE UPON A CHOCOLATE KISS

BY

CHERYL WOLVERTON

Playing Good Samaritan by taking in a stranger after accidentally breaking his foot was the least that Samantha Hampton could do. But would the sweet candy shop owner forgive Richard Moore when she learned he was the son of the competition?

Don't miss

ONCE UPON A CHOCOLATE KISS
On sale November 2003

Available at your favorite retail outlet.

HEART OF STONE

BY

LENORA WORTH

Stone Dempsey had struggled with his faith, but found a kindred spirit and a reason to believe again. Because shy Tara Parnell, a struggling widow with a stubborn streak, entered his world. Would this rugged businessman make the deal of his lifetime—for a bride?

Don't miss

HEART OF STONE
On sale November 2003

Available at your favorite retail outlet.